THIS IS NOT A TEST

ALSO BY COURTNEY SUMMERS

Fall for Anything
Some Girls Are
Cracked Up to Be

THIS IS NOT A TEST

COURTNEY SUMMERS

 ST. MARTIN'S GRIFFIN 🐾 NEW YORK

This is a work of fiction. All of the characters, organizations, and events portrayed in this novel are either products of the author's imagination or are used fictitiously.

www.stmartins.com

Design by Anna Gorovoy

Library of Congress Cataloging-in-Publication Data

Summers, Courtney.
  This is not a test / Courtney Summers.
     p. cm.
  Summary: Barricaded in Cortege High with five other teens while zombies try to get in, Sloane Price observes her fellow captives become more unpredictable and violent as time passes although they each have much more reason to live than she has.
  ISBN 978-0-312-65674-4 (pbk)
  ISBN 978-1-250-01181-7 (e-book)
  [1. Survival—Fiction. 2. Zombies—Fiction. 3. Family problems—Fiction. 4. High schools—Fiction. 5. Schools—Fiction. 6. Horror stories.] I. Title.
  PZ7.S95397Thi 2012
  [Fic]—dc23

                                                    2012004633

First Edition: June 2012

10   9   8   7   6   5   4   3   2   1

This book is for David Summers.

"It is not my expectation to change the world.
I want to change my life."

I love and miss you, Dad.

THIS IS NOT A TEST

Lily,
I woke up and the last piece of my heart disappeared.
I opened my eyes and I felt it go.

I sit on the edge of the bathtub and run the fingernail of my thumb up the inside of my wrist. I trace a vein until it pitchforks out and disappears under the fleshiest part of my palm. Lily couldn't sleep; a few weeks before she left, she had all these pills to help her do that. I didn't know why at the time but now I think her guilt was probably keeping her up at night. When I searched her bedroom earlier, I couldn't find them, which is too bad. I was counting on it. Her. I should know better. It just seemed like maybe the stars would align for this—that the day I decided to die, everything would go right. But they didn't and now I'm not sure what I'll do.

Three sharp raps on the bathroom door—*onetwothree*—stop me breathing. I look up from my wrist. I didn't hear his footsteps. I never hear them when it matters anymore, but I hear them now, retreating down the hall. I wait a few minutes before leaving the bathroom and then I walk the same path downstairs he did. His cologne soaks the air, musky and cheap, and the scent is so heavy in my lungs it makes me want to tear my skin off. It's stronger the closer I get to the kitchen and mingles with a more bitter scent: burnt toast. He burned the toast. He only does that when he thinks I deserve it. I check my watch.

I am five minutes late for breakfast.

Early morning light streams in through the window above the sink. Everything it touches turns gold. Everything looks golden, but it all feels so gray. An envelope sits next to my plate of (burnt) toast. I pick it up and run my fingers along the edge of it as my father explains it's for the school, about my absence. His cover. This is what we are going to tell them kept me home for so long: I had that flu that's going around. Do I understand? I had the flu.

He says, "Let me get a look at your face."

I tilt my chin up. It's not good enough. In one swift motion, he reaches across the table and I flinch away before I can stop myself. He exhales impatiently, takes my chin in his hand, and turns it roughly toward the light. I keep my eyes on the envelope, like I could turn it into a letter from Lily just by looking at it. A letter that says, *hey, I'm coming back for you tonight.* I used to read the actual note she left me over and over again and I'd pretend those words were coded between the ones that said *I'm so sorry* and *I can't do this anymore.*

He lets go of my chin.

Things got worse after you left.

How it is now: my father's face, buried in the newspaper. My mother buried six feet underground. My sister, Lily, gone. Two charred pieces of toast set out before me. I forgot the butter, left it on the counter next to the fridge. I want it badly, but once I'm at the table, I'm not allowed to leave until my plate is clean.

Mornings like this, I remember that one and only sleepover at Grace Casper's house. Waking up with her the next day, scampering downstairs before we were even dressed. The radio blared the news and her mother and father raised their voices over it to be heard. They had an entire conversation this way. Her brother, Trace, turned the TV on over the radio—it was so much noise—and I was too overwhelmed to eat and no one got mad at me for it. Grace said she could tell by the look on my face it was different at my place and she asked me what it was like and I lied to her. I said it was the same, just slightly quieter.

What it really is is silent except for the clock ticking on the wall, reminding me I have only three minutes left to eat. My father flips to the classifieds. Two minutes. Past them. One minute. Folds the paper. Time. He peers at me and the still uneaten toast.

"You better eat that," he says.

The edge in his voice closes my throat. I pick at a snag in my fingernail and peel it sideways, trying to open my airways by distracting my body with new pain. Blood prickles at the corner of my thumb but it doesn't work, I still can't swallow, so I start to pray instead. I pray for something, anything to happen so I don't have to eat this toast because I can't eat this toast. I wasn't raised to believe in God but Lily is gone and I'm all that's left and I never ask for anything. Maybe that counts for something.

"But what if—" The words die as soon as they leave my mouth. "I'm not . . ."

He stares at me.

"If I'm not—what if I'm not . . . hungry . . ."

"You know we don't waste food in this house."

And then, something:

Our front door starts to rattle and shake.

My father lowers the paper slightly.

"HELP! Help us, please—"

The sound sends shock waves through the room. A girl, screaming. The door continues to rattle, the doorknob turns frantically left and right. I stand before I realize what I'm doing. I stand before my plate is clear. The pounding stops as abruptly as it started but I heard it, I know I did. There was a girl out there. She needs help.

"Sit down," my father says.

"But—"

"*Now.*"

I sit. My father slaps the paper onto the table and nods sharply at my plate, which is as good as telling me it better be empty when he comes back. He leaves the room to investigate, swearing under his breath, but before he does I think I see him hesitate and I have never seen him hesitate in my life. I stare at the toast and forget about the girl because it doesn't matter what's happening outside. I have to eat. I can't eat. I hurry across the kitchen. I dump the toast in the garbage and cover it with a crumpled napkin and then I throw myself back into my seat and try to look normal, calm. If he sees what I've done on my face, his face will purple. His lips will thin. He'll say, *we have to talk about this now*. But we won't. Talk, that is.

Times like these, I need Lily. Whenever I'm about to get in trouble, Lily is (was) the one who reminds (reminded) me to breathe. I try to imagine her next to me, whispering in my ear, but it doesn't work because now whenever I think of her, I think of her six months ago, slipping that letter under my door, slipping out of the house, slipping into the beat-up old Volkswagen she bought when she was sixteen, slipping out of my life. I wonder where she ran to, where she's hiding. If our money's gone. If she's spent it all by now.

Now I'm leaving too.

The sound of sirens closes in on our street. I want to look out the window but if he finds me at the window that would be bad. The front door slams shut. Dad storms into the room and I jump from my chair so fast it goes flying into the cupboards. I lose myself in endless apologies—*I'm sorry, I couldn't eat it, I know it's a waste, I'm so sorry*—but he's screaming over me and his voice is so loud and so panicked at first I can't understand a word he's saying.

And there's blood on him.

"—*go, we have to go!*—"

I see the blood and my head is full of snapshots: the coffee table. My head against it. Blood in my hair. The floor mashed against my face. My teeth mashed against my lips. Later, more bruises than I could count. I don't know what he's done this time, what's happened, but I don't want to be part of it. I push past my father and rush down the hall to the front door. I struggle with the chain lock. Slide it out of place. I pull the door open and—

Tires squealing against the pavement.

People running directionless.

Screaming.

This must be a dream. I must not be awake. Or I'm awake and someone ruined our tidy, quiet street while we were sleeping. Broken glass. Doors flung wide open. Cars parked and running with no one inside of them. An alarm sounds nearby. Smoke billows out the window of a house down the street. Mr. North's house. A police car is parked haphazardly on his lawn, its lights flashing. A fire. That must be what's happened except I can't understand why this would turn everyone to panic.

Everyone is panicking.

People rush by. They don't even look at me. A loud *crack* makes me jump but I can't source the sound. Another scream. A group of people run down the road, so frenzied their movements are jerky and uncontrolled. I watch one of them fall, a man. The others surround him, they're so desperate to pull him to his feet they overwhelm him and I can't tell where he stops and they begin.

A car careens past and takes out our mailbox but it keeps going. I take a few dumb steps down the walk and spot a woman staggering awkwardly across our lawn. Is this the girl that needed help? She is covered in red, half hunched over, her arms reaching for someone I can't see. I don't know who she is, but I call out to her; I want to know if the blood on my father is hers. She somehow hears me over all the other noises and turns her head in my direction at the same time my father grabs me and yanks me back inside, throwing me into the foyer. I hit the wall as he slams the door shut—in the woman's face. I glimpse a crimson-stained mouth just before the sound of her body colliding against the wood fills the house. My father takes me by the arm and drags me down the hall. He walks so fast, I can't keep up. I trip and land on my knees. He whirls around. I cover my face with my hands instinctively but he hoists me to my feet and drags me toward the door to the rec room—

An awful sound explodes from the living room.

Our picture window breaking into a thousand pieces.

He lets me go and doubles back. "Get in the rec room, Sloane, and *don't move!*"

Get in the rec room. Move. Don't move. *Move.* I crawl after him, crawl until I see the living room carpet glittering in the sunlight. Glass is everywhere. I watch the woman who was on our lawn writhe through our window, oblivious to the leftover shards and blades of it digging into her legs and hands. She streaks blood on the white sill and as soon as she's through, steadies herself on our pale yellow couch. She leaves a red handprint in her wake. She doesn't even look like she knows where she is. She pauses, rolls her shoulders and inhales. The air rattles through her lungs and makes me breathless. Her head jerks left to right, left to right, left to right before stopping abruptly. She looks at us, takes us in.

She lunges.

It's easy for my father to overpower her. Because she's nothing, she's small, he pins her by the neck with one hand and, with the other, gropes around for something to defend himself with. She gnashes her teeth and claws at his arms so hard she breaks skin, makes him bleed, and the blood makes her wild. She twists her head toward it. My father finds a large piece of broken glass and raises it above him.

He thrusts it into her chest.

And then he does it again.

Again.

The woman doesn't realize she's supposed to be dying. It's like she's becoming more alive, stronger each time the glass is forced into her. She fights to free herself against my father's waning grip and he stabs blindly until finally, desperately, he drives the glass into her left eye and the woman stops moving.

She's stopped moving.

He stares at her body and sits there, drenched in someone else's life, and he looks so calm, like he knew this was coming, like the way this morning started it was only ever going to end up like this. The room starts to spin.

"Sloane," he says.

I find my way to my feet and back into the hall, knocking into the end table where we keep the phone. It clatters to the floor. The sound of the dial tone steadies me, rights the earth.

"Sloane—"

I push through the front door again and I keep moving until I reach the sidewalk. I'm just in time to see two cars meet in the middle of my street but not in time to get between them. The raw crunch of metal sends me reeling back and puts everything on pause for one brief, critical moment where I edge around the wreckage and try to focus on one thing that makes sense. This: Mr. Jenkins is spread-eagle on his lawn, in his housecoat. He's twitching. Mrs. Jenkins is kneeling over him. She rips his shirt wide open. *Heart attack,* I think. Mr. Jenkins has a bad heart. *She's giving him CPR.*

Except that's not what it is at all.

Mrs. Jenkins's determined fingers have torn past the material of Mr. Jenkins's shirt.

And now they are tearing into his chest.

PART ONE

SEVEN DAYS LATER

"Get the door! Get the tables against the fucking door, Trace—*move!*"

In a perfect world, I'm spinning out. I'm seven days ago, sleeping myself into nothingness. Every breath in and out is shallower than the last until, eventually, I stop. In a perfect world, I'm over. I'm dead. But in this world, Lily took the pills with her and I'm still alive. I'm climbing on-stage before Cary notices and gives me something to do even though I should be doing something. I should help. I should be helping because seconds are critical. He said this over and over while we ran down streets, through alleys, watched the community center fall, hid out in empty houses and he was right—seconds are critical.

You can lose everything in seconds.

"Harrison, Grace, take the front! Rhys, I need you in the halls with me—"

I slip past the curtain. I smell death. It's all over me but it's not me, not yet. I am not dead yet. I run my hands over my body, feeling for something that doesn't belong. We were one street away and they came in at all sides with their arms out, their hands reaching for me with the kind of sharp-teethed hunger that makes a person—them. Cary pulled me away before I could have it, but I thought—I thought I felt something, maybe—

"Sloane? Where's Sloane?"

I can't reach far enough behind my back.

"Rhys, the halls—"

"Where is she?"

"We have to get in the halls *now*!"

"Sloane? *Sloane!*"

I look up. Boxy forms loom overhead, weird and ominous. Stage lights. And I don't know why but I dig my cell phone out of my pocket and I dial Lily. If this is it, I want her to know. I want her to hear it. Except her number doesn't work anymore, hasn't worked since she left, and I don't know how I forgot that. I can't believe I forgot that. Instead of Lily, that woman's voice is in my ear: *Listen closely.* She sounds familiar, like someone's mother. Not my mother. I was young when she died. Lily was older. Car accident . . .

"*Sloane!*" Rhys pushes the curtain back and spots me. I drop the phone. It clatters to the floor. "What the hell are you doing? We've got to move—" He takes in the look on my face and his turns to ash. "Are you bit? Did you get bitten?"

"I don't know—" I unbutton my shirt and pull it off and I know he sees all of me before I can turn away, but I don't care. I have to know. "I can't see anything—I can't feel it—"

Rhys runs his hands over my back, searching for telltale marks. He murmurs prayers under his breath while I hold mine.

"It's okay—you're good—you're fine—you're alive—"

The noises in the auditorium get louder with the frantic scrambling of people who actually want to live, but I'm still.

I'm good, I'm fine.

"Are you sure?"

"I'm sure—now come on—come on, we have to—"

Good, fine. I'm fine. I'm fine, I'm fine. He grabs my arm. I shrug him off and put my shirt back on more slowly than I should. I am fine. I'm alive.

I don't even know what that means.

"Look, we've got to get back out there," he says as I do up my buttons. "There are three other doors that need to be secured—" He grabs my arm and turns me around. "Look at me—are you ready? Sloane, are you ready?"

I open my mouth but nothing comes out.

This must be what Dorothy felt like, I think. Maybe. If Dorothy was six scared teenagers and Oz was hell. No, this must be a joke; we are six scared teenagers and our high school is one of the last buildings in Cortege that is still in one piece and I'm not sure I can think of a better or worse place to spend the end of days. It was supposed to be the community center. We went there first like we were told—the town's designated emergency shelter for the kind of emergencies we were assured would likely never happen—and it was the first place to fall. There were too many of us and too many of them. Somehow, we fought our way from one side of town to the other. In another life, the trip would have taken forty minutes.

In this one, it took seven days.

"Listen closely."

The radio crackles the prerecorded voice of that woman at us over and over. We have done everything she has told us to do. We have locked and barricaded all the doors. We have covered the windows so no one can see outside and—more importantly—nothing can see in. *"Do not draw attention to yourself,"* the woman says, but if we know anything by now, it's that. *"Once you have found a secure location, stay where you are and help will come soon."* Cary sits on the stage across from me, waiting for the message to change. It doesn't.

"This is not a test. Listen closely. This is not a test."

But I think she's wrong. I think this is a test.

It has to be.

Grace and Trace sit on the floor below. She's whispering in his ear and he's nodding to whatever she's saying and he doesn't look right. He looks sick. He reaches for his sister's hand and holds it tightly, pressing his fingers into her skin like he's making sure she exists. After a while, he feels me looking at him and turns his pale face in my direction. I hold his gaze until the chaos outside breaks my concentration. Outside, where everything is falling, landing and breaking at once. Sometimes you catch something specific like the screams and cries of people trying to hold on to each other before they're swallowed into other, bigger noises.

This is what it sounds like when the world ends.

I take in the auditorium. The cheery purple and beige walls, the matching banners that hang from the ceiling, the Rams posters (GO RAMS, GO!) taped up all over. It was Cary's idea to come to the school. After we found the community center overrun, we heard that woman's voice on the phone. *Find a place.* He didn't even hesitate before he said *CHS.* Cortege High. It was built to be the most distraction-free learning environment in the county, which means maximum windows for minimal view. Strategically placed transoms line the classrooms and halls, save for skylights in the auditorium and gym. Two large windows open up the right side of the second and third floors and overlook the school's parking lot. They're covered now.

"It's still happening," Harrison says.

I follow his tearful gaze to the exit just right of the stage. The doors open into the parking lot which bleeds out into the streets of Cortege, a half-dead, half-dying town. They're locked, the doors. Locked and covered with lunch tables reinforced by desks, thanks to Rhys and me. Every entrance and exit in here is the same. The idea is nothing gets past these barriers we've created. We spent the first five hours here putting them up. We've spent the last two shaking and quiet, waiting for them to fall.

"Of course it's still happening," Rhys mutters. "Why wouldn't it be?"

Cary turns the radio off and eases himself onto the floor. He looks like he has something to say but first he runs his hands through his black hair, letting his eyes travel over each of us. Cary Chen. We followed *him* for days. Lily used to buy pot from him sometimes and sometimes I wanted to, but I thought that would make English class weird and I don't know if she always paid in cash.

"Listen, I—" He sounds sandpaper rough from screaming instructions at us for hours and never once taking a breath. He clears his throat. "Phone?"

Trace makes a gurgling noise, digs his hand into his pocket, pulls out his cell, and frantically dials a number, but it's no use. The woman's voice drones over each desperate push of the buttons, a condensed version of what we're getting on the radio. I watch the sound work its way into Trace's bones, his blood. His face turns white and he whips his phone across the room. It breaks into three pieces; the back flies off, the battery falls out, and the body skitters across the shiny linoleum floor. Nothing works anymore and the things that still do don't work like they should.

"I can't get through," he says flatly.

Cary picks up the pieces and fits them back in place.

"Give it more time. You will."

"Think they'd pick up if I did?"

I watch Cary, waiting to see if he'll defend himself. He doesn't. He turns the cell phone over and over in his hands and says, "Trace, the message is a good thing. I think it means they're leaving priority signal for emergency workers."

Harrison sniffs. "So they can save us?"

"Yeah." Cary nods. "We'll be saved."

"And that's your expert opinion?" Trace asks.

Cary shrugs but he doesn't look Trace in the eyes, focusing instead on the doors. His expression reveals nothing, but he's turning the phone in his hands faster now, clumsily.

"It just makes sense," he says.

"That's what you said about coming here. That really paid off for me and Grace."

Cary winces.

"He got the rest of us here," Rhys says.

There were eight of us, before.

"Oh, so I'm here. Hey, Grace!" Trace turns to her. "You're *here*. We're *here* with *Cary Chen*." He laughs bitterly. "You think that means *anything* to us when—"

"Trace, stop." Grace sounds just broken enough that Trace doesn't take it any further. He frowns, holds out his hand to Cary and says, "Give me back my fucking phone."

Cary stares at it like he doesn't want to give it up, like Trace's cell phone is an anchor keeping him here but I don't know why anyone would want to be anchored here.

"Now," Trace says.

Cary holds it out and finally looks Trace in the eyes.

"I'm sorry," he says, "about your parents."

Trace rips the phone from Cary's grasp.

I close my eyes and imagine this place under totally normal circumstances. We have assemblies here. The principal gives speeches here. We eat in this room at lunch. I imagine a day, any school day, setting up the lunch tables and getting in line, picking from the menu. I can almost smell the food . . .

But then the noises outside get louder than anything I can imagine. They pump through my veins, speed up my heart, and remind me to be afraid even though I have never stopped being afraid, not since Lily left. I open my eyes at the same time the whole barricade seems to shift. Rhys rushes to it, pushing against the desks and tables until they're settled again.

"What was that?" Harrison asks. "Why did it—"

"It's just the way this desk was—it wasn't the door—"

"It's the *door*?"

"It *wasn't* the door. Just calm down, Harrison. Jesus."

Harrison starts to cry. He stands in the middle of the room and holds himself because no one else will and it's the loneliest thing I've ever seen. I'd go to him, maybe, but I don't even know Harrison. None of us do. He's one of those invisible freshmen made even more invisible by the fact he just moved here four weeks ago. Cary had to ask him his name after we found him trapped under a bike with his jeans caught in the spokes.

Things I know about Harrison now: not only is he short and stocky, he also cries. A lot. Grace takes pity on him because she's better than I'll ever be. She wraps her arm around him and murmurs gentle-sounding words at him and I watch his sobs slowly turn to gasps that turn into pathetic little hiccups. Everyone else averts their eyes. They find things to do so they don't have to watch. I watch because I don't know what else to do. I watch until I can't anymore. I dig my hand into my pockets. My fingers curl around a crumpled piece of paper.

I take it out and unfold it.

Lily,

"Hey."

The voice is quiet, close. I shove the note back in my pocket. Rhys hovers at the edge of the stage. His brown hair sticks up everywhere and his brown eyes are bloodshot. Things I know about Rhys: he's a senior. Our lockers are across from each other.

He put his hands on me and told me I was okay.

He has a case of water in his arms. He sets it on the stage and holds a bottle out to me. I don't even ask him where he got it, just rip it from his hands. I remember us huddled around this old birdbath yesterday, yesterday morning. We cupped our palms together and lapped up all the dirty, stagnant water and it tasted so awful but so, *so* wonderful because we were so desperate and isn't everything better when you're desperate? We managed to forget our parched mouths and cracked lips while we secured the school and settled into the last two hours, but now I don't even know how that's possible because I am so fucking thirsty. I down the water quickly and then I want more. Rhys hands me another and watches me drink it too. I drink until I feel like the ocean is in my stomach and when I'm done, I'm spent. I curl my knees up to my chin and wrap my arms around them. Rhys gives me a crooked smile.

"Still here," he says. "We made it."

"Is that *water*?" Trace calls from his side of the room. "Is that really water?"

I turn my face to the doors.

Sloane.

I jolt awake, forget where I am for a second. Everyone is laid out around me, asleep on the dusty blue gym mats we dragged in from the storage room. The last thing we had energy for, the last thing we could do for ourselves before we totally crashed.

I raise my head and listen.

It's just deep breathing, the noises outside, and nothing else.

I listen hard, but there's nothing else.

I pull at the collar of my shirt and rest my head against the mat. My clothes feel scratchy and awful against my skin, which is covered in a layer of sweat. I force my eyes shut and drift or maybe it's sleep and then I think I hear him again—*Sloane*—and I jerk awake again and this time, when I close my eyes I see the living room floor covered in little pieces of red glass.

After a while, I give up on sleep. I check my watch. It's almost six a.m. I have to pee. My muscles protest as I edge off the mat. The floor is cold and my toes curl in on themselves. I cross the room and step into the hall. It's an open mouth that forks off in different directions. The tiled floors shine weirdly under the emergency lights lining the ceiling. They wash out the uninterrupted stretch of beige and purple walls and make them almost seem to glow. I feel like a ghost underneath them. The robot beep that happens just before an announcement comes over the loudspeakers drifts through my head. It's that woman on the phone and on the radio and she wants us all to *listen closely*. I imagine this place crowded with students, all our faces tilted up. Everything about this is wrong. This school was never built to be empty.

Maybe it's not safe to be out here alone.

Maybe I should go back and wake someone up.

I don't.

If anything happens, it will just happen to me.

I push through the doors to the girls' room and head

straight for the sinks where I'm sick. The sound of myself retching makes me retch more. The only way I get myself to stop is by forcing myself to straighten before I'm finished. Bile dribbles down my chin. I twist the faucets without thinking.

Water.

Water. Comes. Out.

Does everyone know this? Did they find out before me? I avoided the taps when I was in here before because I didn't want to end up disappointed if they didn't work but they work and no one said a word to me about it. *Running water.* I stare at the gushing faucet for too long and then I hold my hands under the stream and splash my face, my neck. Dip my wet hands below my shirt. My body trembles in gratitude but I have no idea who to thank. I turn the faucet off and then I turn it on again just to be sure of what I saw, that I didn't imagine it.

I *didn't* imagine it.

The water is real. It moves effortlessly from spout to drain.

I turn it off. I use the toilet. When I come out of the stall, I'm confronted by something else I've managed to avoid. My reflection. My skin is tinged green and my brown hair is greasy, strands all clumped together, hanging around my face. There's a bruise directly below my right eye and I'm not sure how it got there. I trace it with my fingertips. I look better than I did three weeks ago. Funny. The end of the world has done less damage to my face.

I laugh. I lean against the sink and laugh so hard my sides split and I die and it's good. I press my hands against the mirror. Over my face. The glass feels weird and unreal against my palms. If you break glass into pieces, you can use one of those pieces as a highly effective weapon against another human being. Right through the eye. I saw it. I saw it, I did, I saw it. I stare at my fingernails. They're ruined, cracked. Rhys and Cary found me sitting in the middle of the road, six streets away from my home, digging my fingernails into the pavement. They thought I was trying to get to my feet, that I wanted to keep going when really I was just waiting to die because I thought I had actually found Lily's pills and taken them and my brain was inventing this weird dreamscape before it finally shut down for good because how could this be real? How could it be true? The dead don't just come back to life.

By the time I realized it was real, it was true, it was too late to tell Cary and Rhys I wasn't like them. That I didn't want to keep going. They were working so hard to hold on, I knew they wouldn't understand. So I stayed with them.

Mostly because I didn't think we'd make it this far.

I reenter the auditorium as quietly as I exited it and lay on my mat. Rhys is on my left, facing away from me. His gray shirt is splattered with dirt and blood. Trace is on my right, on his back, his mouth hanging open. I stare at the skylights overhead until weak rays of sun filter in. A new day. If what I hear beyond them is any indication, it's the same as the last.

Someone stirs. Cary. First awake, not counting myself. So strange. I think of him in English class at the back of the room; how he listened with his head in his arms and answered all of Mr. Baxter's questions in the same unhurried way: *I don't know,* and how he couldn't afford to because he was repeating eleventh grade and didn't he just want out of here like the rest of us? I close my eyes but he tiptoes his way over to me—no, Rhys. He wakes Rhys and they soft-shoe across the room. I hear the slight jangle of the keys he stole from Principal LaVallee's office and then the sound of the kitchen door gliding open and closed.

I open my eyes. Trace is next to show signs of life. His eyes flicker back and forth beneath his eyelids and he moans, curling his fingers into fists. His whole body tenses until he shouts himself awake, bolting upright before collapsing back on his mat, sweaty and shaking. Grace is next to him in a heartbeat. He grabs her hand, eyes still shut, chest heaving. But he doesn't—can't—speak.

"It's okay," she whispers. "I'm here."

The way she says it, the way she's beside him—I want to be between them. I want to be in the direct path of their togetherness so I can steal some of the feeling for myself. Grace's eyes drift from Trace to me and I look away, self-conscious. Grace is beautiful. Dirty and covered in blood, she is so beautiful. Prettier than me. But that shouldn't matter, I guess.

Harrison is last awake. He sits up and rubs his eyes, digging his fists into them. He does this for so long I wonder if he might need someone to tell him to stop until I realize he's trying to cover up the fact he's crying. Wasted effort. When he finally lowers his hands and notices the two empty gym mats, he freaks.

"Where are they?" He twists around. "Where did they—"

The kitchen door swings open. Cary and Rhys march

into the room, each carrying trays loaded with food. I sit up and watch as they set them in front of our mats and I see bagels and apples and bananas and rice cakes and globs of peanut butter and jam packets on plates surrounded by plastic cutlery. Juice and water. I'm *hungry*. I crawl over to the tray and Grace and Harrison follow suit. The bananas are browning so I reach for an apple instead.

"Eat slowly or you might make yourself sick," Rhys says.

Cary takes a bagel, tears a piece off and dips it in jam. He pops it in his mouth, closes his eyes and relishes that first bite.

"We're set up for a while, food-wise," he says, swallowing.

"How long is a while?" I ask.

"I'm sure help will come before we eat it all."

I stare at my apple, pressing my fingers against it just to make sure it's real. It's solid, cold. I sink my teeth into its waxy skin and it's sweet enough to make my eyelids flutter. Next to me, Rhys drinks an entire bottle of orange juice in one go, crunching the plastic in his fist when he's finished.

"Water's still going," he says. "So that's good."

No one else seems surprised about the water except Harrison, so I guess they all knew about this incredible thing but none of them thought to tell me. And I think I'd be mostly okay with that if I was in anyone's company but Harrison's.

"But the power's off," Harrison says.

"Water tank on top of the school," Cary says. "I think we should have enough until this whole thing blows over, but that doesn't mean we shouldn't conserve—like, no obsessive-compulsive hand-washing, that kind of thing . . ."

Harrison's eyes bug. "You think it'll blow over?"

Grace reaches for an apple and holds it out to Trace.

"You should eat," she says.

"You really think it will blow over?"

"I'm not hungry," Trace mutters.

"Do you think it will blow over?" Harrison demands, but we're all watching Trace and Grace now and they know we're watching them and that makes it worse.

"Please."

"No."

"For me."

"I said no."

"Trace, you need to—"

"I said I'm not *fucking* hungry!"

I twitch. Trace is so close, he might as well be yelling at me and I hate it when people yell at me. I hate the silence after. This silence, after. I raise the apple to my lips to distract myself from it, but its sickly sweet smell suddenly turns my stomach. I set it down.

"Cary," Harrison says. "Do you think it'll—"

"*Yes,* Harrison."

It's quiet until Rhys clears his throat.

"Doors are secure. What else do we need to do today?"

"Well." Cary. "I was thinking—"

"Wait." Trace.

"What?"

"If Rhys asked *us* what *we* need to do today, then why are *you* answering?"

Cary stares at Trace.

"Forget it. Never mind."

Harrison's eyes dart between them. "I want to know what Cary was going to say."

"I do too," Rhys says.

"I don't think Trace wants to hear it."

"No, I just wanted to know why *you* get to be *our* voice. You just jumped right in there and spoke for all of us. So what are you, like—leader, now?"

"Holy shit." Cary raises his hands. "Nobody said anything about leading—"

"I mean, I'm not going to stand in your way or anything, since we know what happens to people who you seem to think are disposable—"

"*Christ*, Trace," Rhys says.

"Oh, sorry, Moreno. I forgot you were president of the Cary Chen Fan Club since he got *most* of us here and everything."

The whole time Trace is talking, my eyes are on Cary. I don't have to look at Trace to know the vein in his forehead is pulsing, that he's talking through his teeth. Cary's face is deceptively calm but his eyes are all sadness. Maybe guilt.

"Say what you want to say, Trace," he says.

"Okay, fine. There was no way in *hell* that alley went from empty to swarmed in ten seconds. You said it was clear—"

"They move fast—it *was* clear—"

"You said it was clear and you *knew* it wasn't and you let them walk *right into it*—"

"It was clear!"

I flinch again. Cary gets to his feet and Trace does the same. I have this vision of Trace killing Cary, straddling him on the auditorium floor, bashing his head against it until Cary's brains are everywhere. Cary sees it too. He walks away like that's the end of it, but then he doubles back, red-faced, and points at Trace. His fingers are in the shape of a gun.

"I would have never, *never*—"

"But you did. You *know* you did—"

"Trace, what could Cary have *possibly* gained by doing that?" Rhys asks.

Trace turns on him. "I *know* what I saw—"

"Did anyone else see it? Hey, Sloane, did you see it? Did you see Cary tell the Caspers to walk into a swarmed alley? What did you see?" I shake my head, trying to keep myself from being pulled into this but he won't stop. "Come on, tell us what you saw, Sloane—" The more he says it the more I feel myself start to cave—*I'll tell Rhys what I saw, no, I'll say what Trace wants to hear*—when two things happen: Grace screams, *"Stop!"* At the same time a loud *bang* sounds against the doors, startling us all, sending us scrambling back.

We stare at the doors for the longest time after that but nothing else happens.

Harrison whispers, "Oh no," over and over even though nothing else happens.

"Look," Cary finally says, and he sounds tired, like it's the end of a long day and not the start of new one. "We should check the barricades. Maybe add more to them and make sure nothing's moved. That's all I was going to say before."

"I am *not* helping you," Trace says.

He storms across the room, his footsteps loud against the floor, somehow louder than everything that's going on outside. He steps into the hall like he has somewhere to go but there's nowhere to go.

I think of reality TV shows.

Contestants on an island, whatever. This feels like it could be bad reality television. I imagine an audience, comfortable at home, some other world watching this right now, judging me for everything I've done and will do. This is television. We're actors pretending to be people and when this is all over, one of us will be a million dollars richer. I just forgot.

I look around and try to spot the hidden cameras.

Nothing.

We've split up to check the barricades. Cary takes the front doors, Rhys takes the back. Harrison is looking after the exit in the library and Grace volunteers for the gym. That leaves me with the auditorium ("Just check for weaknesses," Rhys told me), staring at all the tables and desks. I don't touch them. The doors will stay shut or they won't.

I'm not alone long. Trace comes back.

"What did you see?" he asks.

He heads straight for the stage, for the tray of leftover food. He picks through it before settling on what Grace first offered him—an apple. He tears into it and I watch the ecstasy of that first bite on his face, taste it with my lips as his mouth makes its way around the fruit.

When he's finished, he sets the core back on the tray.

"What did you see?" he asks again. I press my lips together. "What, you're not gonna speak to me?"

"It doesn't matter what I saw."

"It does to me."

Trace is Grace's twin, but there's nothing of his sister in him, not really. She's curvy and soft—kind of vintage pretty—and he's solid in a way that comes from playing one sport too many. His brown eyes are hard, but they can be warm and teasing, like that time I slept over. They're not like that now. He looks away from me.

"Think they're dead?"

"I don't know."

I don't want to think about it. I don't want to think about Mr. and Mrs. Casper disappearing into a horde of infected. Even as they were being pulled away from us, they were reaching for their children and Trace and Grace reached back because they didn't want to be left. And then they were gone. It's wrong. The Caspers are the only real family I've ever known and they were torn apart through no choice of their own. They wanted to be together.

I think that's enough reason for them to still be together. It's stupid, how it works out sometimes.

"They were totally outnumbered," Trace says.

"I know."

So was I, for a minute. Hands, faces, open mouths, milky white eyes. All that disease free-flowing under their skin, trying to force its way into mine. I hold my arms out, look at the skin that's exposed, that was exposed, and wonder how much of them is still on me. I rub my hands over my arms, slowly at first, and then fast, faster. I itch. A word I forgot existed enters my head: *shower*. I can *smell* myself. I smell all of the dirt, the sweat, going to the bathroom when there was no place to go, the blood I got on me that's dried now—

Trace stares. "What the hell is wrong with you?"

I pull at my shirt. The cotton plaid is stained red and brown. Rhys's voice is in my head, from yesterday, taunting me: *Still here still here still here still here.*

"God, look at us," I say. "It's all over us—"

The locker rooms are on the other side of the school.

I have to pass Rhys at the back doors to get to them. He's adding a storage cupboard from Mrs. Lafferty's room to a mountain of other furniture and he doesn't notice me slip by. I find a spare set of clothes in my locker. I hold them to my face and inhale, hoping for the scent of something familiar and comforting—like how I used to just stand in Lily's room after she left and breathe her in—but they only smell like school.

I take my suicide note out of my pocket and set it carefully on the top shelf, fighting the urge to shove it in my mouth so I'll feel less empty. I don't know how I'm going to do this, move through the hours like someone who wants to still be breathing when I had so firmly made up my mind to stop. I'm not supposed to be here and the world has ended and it's too stupid and sad for words and it's changed time; a second is a minute, a minute is an hour, an hour is a day, a day is a month, a month is a year, and a year—

I can't be here that long.

When I step into the locker rooms, I hear myself move twice, like I'm made of echoes. The light is better in here. The sun spills in from the transoms and makes everything seem peaceful. I walk over to them and get on my tiptoes but I can't see anything except sky and then I start thinking about people in space, astronauts, and if they're just stuck up there forever trying to reach everyone here on earth, getting no answer and not knowing why and I think that would be horrible, but good—the not knowing. I wouldn't want to know. I stay like that for a long time when the door opens. Grace steps inside and I hear a bell somewhere, I swear. Post-PE, time to shower. But it's not those days anymore, so the second thing my mind reaches for is something's wrong.

"Trace told me about your idea." She's hugging a bundle of clothes to her chest. "I told everyone else. Cary said ten minutes tops with the water."

Grace is all good words. Nice, generous, great listener. The kind of student government president the student body votes in for all the right reasons. She unfolds the clothes in her arms and holds up a dress. I recognize it from the school's production of *West Side Story*.

"The drama department provides." She eyes my clothes jealously. "I didn't have anything of my own."

For a second, neither of us says anything. Grace and me, I don't know what we are. Almost friends? But then we stopped talking and looking at each other in the halls. It had to happen, I guess, but I always wondered why she was the one who started it when it should have been me. I always secretly wanted to ask her why.

We head to the showers. I don't change out of my clothes until I'm in a stall behind a cheap plastic curtain and then I peel them off slow. Shirt, jeans. I let them stay under my feet. They need to be clean too. I look down at myself. Patches of bruises, scrapes, scratches. I turn the water on. The showerhead sputters once, twice, and then sprays water all over me.

It's *freezing*.

"Shit!" Grace shrieks from the stall beside mine. "Shit, shit, shit, shit, *shit*!"

I twist the hot water knob desperately. Nothing happens. No hot water. None. It seems obvious now but *Jesus*. I run my hands over my body quickly, trying to get as much of the dirt and grime and blood off as possible in the least amount of time. I take measured breaths in and out and pretend the water's warm. Soak my hair. This is awful.

As soon as I feel clean, I turn the water off and lean against the wall, dripping and shivering. I don't think that was ten minutes. Grace is still under the water, so I sprint out naked, grab my clothes, and pull them on. They cling to my damp body. I sit on the bench and wait for her. She takes a while, longer than she should, and when she finally does come out, she's naked. Of course she's naked but she's so—confident. She was like that at our sleepover too. At the end of the night, she changed in front of me and I remember wondering what it would be like to have a body like hers. I wonder it now. She's fleshy and beautiful and I'm so much the opposite of that. I don't have a body that's nice to hold. She slips the dress over her head and runs her fingers through her wet hair. She looks especially vintage now, perfect and untouched.

"Trace thinks maybe they're still alive," she says casually, like she's talking about the weather, clothes, I don't know. I'd almost believe it meant as little to her as any of those things if her face didn't dissolve directly after she said it. She brings her arm to her eyes and cries.

I don't know what to do.

"I can get him if you want," I offer awkwardly.

"*No.* God, I don't want him to see me like this." She lowers her arm and takes short breaths in and out. "I think they're dead. I think they're dead. I have to say it. They're dead. But I don't want Trace to know I think that. I want him to hope."

I bet Lily's safe wherever she is. I bet she found a soldier who took her away to some camp, some survivor camp, and she's in some bunker right now, eating rations. Flirting.

I bet this is all a relief to her.

"You're a good sister," I tell Grace, but I feel very far away when I do.

"Thanks." She wipes at her face. "Uhm, could you just . . . give me a minute?"

"Sure."

We stare at each other.

". . . Alone?"

"Oh. Yeah, sure. Of course."

Before I leave, I want to ask her if she remembers the sleepover in sophomore year. I want to tell her that I was thinking of her when the world ended but I don't.

Later, the emergency lights seem to stop working one by one. Cary says it's a miracle they lasted as long as they did. When Harrison asks him what this means for us, Cary says it'll be harder to move around at night, but that we have enough natural light in the day. We find a few flashlights in the custodian's office to guide us through the darkness and no one points out the obvious—that sooner or later they will run out of battery power too.

Trace wakes everyone up.

He's running circles around the room, his sneakers slap-
ping against the floor. It's a sound that gets steadily more
annoying the longer my eyes are open because of it.

Rhys groans and says what we're all thinking.

"Jesus. I'm trying to fucking sleep here, Trace."

"Before all this shit happened," Trace says, breathless

as he laps us, "I'd wake up by six and do five miles. I'm not stopping for you, Moreno."

"The school has a gym," Cary points out.

"Blow me, you stupid fuck."

"You kiss your mother with that—"

It comes out of Cary's mouth automatically. One of those stupid throw-away lines you just say that you've probably said before except this is not a stupid throw-away line anymore.

Trace stops running.

I can't deal with them fighting so I close my eyes and go back to sleep. The next time I wake up, no one has moved except Trace isn't running anymore. He sits next to Grace on her mat while she fiddles with her phone.

"My battery's dead," she says.

"Doesn't make a difference," Trace says. "I checked the landlines in here. They're out. There's no more emergency message on them. Lasted nine days, though, so I guess that's something."

I close my eyes and go back to sleep. The next time I wake up, it's breakfast. Rice cakes smothered in jam, canned peaches. I stay awake this time but I'm not sure why.

"Zombies," Harrison says.

"Shut the fuck up," Trace tells him.

Rhys laughs. It's a sharp, unpleasant sound at first and then he *really* starts to laugh. He covers his face with his hands, his shoulders shaking, while we stare at him.

"Sorry." He wipes at his eyes. "Just—sorry."

"Do you think it's the government?" Harrison asks,

picking at his mat. "And that it's just local? Like . . . they did this to us?"

"I think they'd have bombed the shit out of us by now if that was the case," Cary says.

"So then it's global," Trace decides. "And if it's global, I doubt anyone's coming for us."

This sets Harrison off. "What? But—"

"The message on the radio is still going," Cary says. "They'll come. This is what I think: Cortege is a small town, right? So it might take them a while to get to us. You think it's crazy here, just imagine how it is in, like, the city or something. We'd have no chance."

"Was anyone here sick?" Rhys asks. "That flu?" No one says anything. Rhys glances at me. "You were out for a while, weren't you? The last couple of weeks before this started. Were you sick?"

"I'm not infected," I say. "Do I look infected to you?"

"I didn't mean that," Rhys says quickly, but I don't know what else he could have meant. "I'm just trying to figure it out."

"I don't think it's the flu," Cary says. "I think that was just weird timing."

"Maybe it's terrorists," Harrison says.

The boys go back and forth for a while, trying to figure out how and why this started, like they have the brainpower to piece it together and if they do, it will change the fact it happened and that we're here. Grace stares up at the skylight and says, "Maybe it's God."

"Don't be so cliché," Trace tells her.

But everyone stops talking about it after that.

"It was almost better when we were out there." Rhys sighs.

"Don't even joke about that," Harrison says.

We're still in the auditorium, lounging. There was lunch and there was napping, long stretches of silence and a bit of arguing. It's barely past three. I understand what Rhys means. Waiting around to be saved is like waiting to die and I have done more of both than anyone else in this room. There's a whole lot of nothing before there's something and running was something.

Everyone clings to the idea of safety and because the auditorium seems safest, no one likes to venture too far from it without someone else in tow. Everyone except me, that is. I say I'm going to the bathroom but instead I wander the school and I pretend I'm walking Cortege when everything was normal, when it looked nice. Four years ago, all this money went into its beautification. Trees were planted along the main street, lights were strung on them, flowerbeds were put in every blank space and we got new street signs, the works.

Now it's gone.

I wonder how much time I have before anyone looks for me. I'm far enough away from the auditorium that I don't hear any voices and I'm far enough away from the entrance that the noises outside seem muted, or maybe they're as loud as they ever are and I'm already used to them. I move past empty offices and classrooms. It's an eerie route that takes me by no one. I reach the stairs to the second floor and pause, suddenly aware my life lacks structure now, that I never have to answer to anybody and I never have to suffer for it. As soon as the thought is in my head, there's another one and it's sharper, clearer, much more painful:

It doesn't change anything.

And then a cheap, musky scent is in the air—a ghost, I know it's a ghost—and my chest aches. I try to remember how to breathe around the loneliness, this being alone, but I can't. I don't know how. I have to climb the stairs to get away from it but there's no getting away from it. I reach the landing and walk the hall, turn the corner. Sun lights this side of the building, save for a large blot of darkness— one of the big windows we covered with poster boards. I walk over and stand in its shade. Press my hand against it.

I wish I could break this window. Step through it. But I can't break this window. I can't even find some less dramatic way to die inside of this school, like hanging myself or slitting my wrists, because what would they do with my body? It might put everyone else at risk. I won't let myself do that.

I'm not selfish like Lily.

I hate her. I hate her so much my heart tries to crawl out of my throat but it gets stuck there and beats crazily in the too narrow space. I bring my hands to my neck and try to massage it back down. I press so hard against the skin, my eyes sting, and then I'm hurrying back down the stairs, back to the first floor. I think of Trace running laps, something he can control.

I push through the bulky gym doors and as soon as

47

they're shut behind me, I run. The bleachers stretch out on either side of the room. Light pours in overhead. The gym used to feel so alive, always bustling, and now it's nothing. The barricade against the exit is monstrous and every time I catch it out of the corner of my eye, my insides jump and it makes me run a little faster until I'm circling the gym at a pace I know I can't maintain, a pace that is killing me. I ran as fast out there, but it was different out there. My body wants more rest, more food.

My body wants to stop.

Thud. I end up on my knees. I'm dripping with sweat and my stomach is churning and the sound I heard was not the sound of myself falling and landing but—*thud.*

I turn my head to the exit.

Thud.

Thud.

Tears stream down Harrison's cheeks.

Thud.

He covers his ears.

Trace and Grace hold hands.

I hold mine together in front of my face, the edges of my thumbs against my lips like I'm praying and I *am* praying. I wasn't raised to believe in God, but sometimes when

I ask for things to happen, they happen. This is what I want to happen: I want the doors to burst open.

"They know we're in here," Rhys says. It's true, they do. They know. This isn't the frenzied sounds of bodies stumbling and tripping against the door amid all the other chaos, an accident that goes away. This is consistent. It has purpose. Intent.

They know we're in here.

"Ours wasn't the most subtle entrance ever," Trace says.

Rhys turns to Grace. "Did you hear this when you checked the barricade yesterday?"

"No. I mean—" She stops and bites her lip. "I don't know? It was really noisy."

"I didn't hear them in here when I put the barricade up," Cary says. "So if we didn't hear them then and Grace didn't hear them yesterday . . ." He trails off. "It means they've figured out we're in here *since* we got in here."

"But how do they know?" Rhys asks.

"Why don't you go out there and ask them?"

"Go to hell, Trace."

"What if it's help?" Harrison asks in a small voice.

No one says anything because we all know it's not help. If it was anyone we wanted inside, they'd use their voice. They'd tell us to open the door. Cary's hand covers his mouth as he thinks. We watch him think. After a while, he starts walking, gesturing us out of the gym. We follow him down the halls until he gets to the very back of the school, to the doors Rhys secured. We stand there and stare at them. Wait.

Thud.

Harrison moans and I wonder what it's like to be him, to feel each bad development like it's the first bad development, that it's still worth resisting enough to cry over.

"Don't start," Cary tells him. "We're not done . . ."

He leads us to the front of the school.

Thud.

The sound of more bodies forcing themselves against the doors, trying to get to us.

We go to home base, the auditorium.

It's started there, too.

Thud.

We finish in the library. We stand there for twenty minutes, none of us speaking, but nothing happens. Here, nothing is outside the door.

"I wonder if they just have to know that we could be in here," Cary says.

Trace snorts. "Bullshit. They *saw* us break in."

"But why didn't we hear them trying to get in before now? Remember that house on Rushmore? We were quiet as hell and they stormed the place."

I remember the house on Rushmore Avenue. It wasn't fortified, not like this, but we were quiet and got inside without being noticed and we stayed quiet. It was only minutes before we were discovered and then we were running again, climbing out a bedroom window while the door holding them back turned to nothing before our eyes. I remember the way it sounded, the wood splintering as easily as a twig . . .

"So you think they want in here because they *can* be in

here? Because the school is here and they are too? That makes no sense, Einstein," Trace says to Cary. "Try again."

"We're practically surrounded," Cary snaps. "If there are no other survivors around this area, what else have they got to do? They're at every fucking door because they're *looking for food.* If anything makes sense to them, it's that buildings like these are just fucking food containers."

"They're not at this door, though," Grace says.

"Why *would* they be at this door?" Cary asks. "It's practically invisible."

"Don't talk to Grace like that," Trace says.

"I wasn't talking to her like anything—"

"Stop," Rhys tells them.

I contemplate the door. The exit in the library opens up into a narrow path that leads around the front of the school and to the athletic field out back. A chain-link fence lines the path, separating the school's property from a dense but small cluster of trees that lead to the road. The front of the path is gated, but the back, leading to the field, is wide open.

"So that's our way out," I say. "If we have to leave."

"That's the door," Cary agrees. "Unless they end up finding it too. In which case, we'd have to fight our way out of here."

Rhys nods. "So we should be ready, one way or the other."

How we are ready:

Two bags packed with the essentials: water, food, clothes, and medical stuff we raided from the nurse's office. Cary and Rhys volunteer to carry them. Trace demands we get a bag each, but changes his mind when he remembers how the dead outside can and will reach for anything they can hold on to. We get aluminum baseball bats from the gym. Our weapons.

The supplies rest on the table next to the door and then we start fine-tuning our plan, as if plans make a difference when you're being chased from one moment to the next. We had a lot of plans before we got here and I'm not sure we saw any of them through.

The plan: if the doors are breached, Cary is counting on the noise of our barricades falling to give us the lead time to get in here and get *this* barricade out of our way. And then we escape into the night. Or the day. Whichever.

Harrison whimpers at the idea of leaving, even though it's purely hypothetical at this point, and we have to promise him repeatedly that we won't leave him behind even though Trace threatens to. When Cary tries to figure out where we'll go after we leave, Trace decides Cary's acting too much like a leader and they get in a fight and we never figure it out. We have this teamwork thing down. And then Cary declares the library off limits.

"We'll check it once a night to see if there's any activity," he says. "But we should keep this part of the school as quiet as possible. I don't know if they can hear us out there, but I *really* don't want to risk it. I want to stay here until we absolutely have to leave."

Which is just another way of saying more waiting.

On the way back to the auditorium, Rhys touches my arm, stopping me. I jerk away, which surprises him but neither of us says anything. Cary turns at the sound of two less people moving with him. Rhys waves like, *just a second.* The others trudge back to the auditorium.

"So, what do you think?" Rhys asks.

I think he's clean. His brown hair isn't spiked with its

own grime. His bangs are sharp against his forehead, some strands longer than others, like he cut his hair himself and he did it in the dark. His face is smooth. The boys have been sharing a razor they found in Coach Hainsworth's office. Rhys Moreno. He used to hang across the street with the other senior smokers until the first bell. Sometimes surrounded by girls, sometimes not.

"What do I think about what?"

"The plan."

I don't tell him there isn't one as far as I'm concerned. As soon as we leave here, I separate from them. Maybe I'll even do something sacrificial so they have time to get away and then I can die a hero or whatever but I've realized something since I got here. I cared too much about how I was going to go before—Lily's pills, the ones I couldn't find—when it doesn't really matter *how* I go, just that I do.

"I mean," he continues. "I don't know. You barely talk."

"Maybe I've got nothing to say."

"Not with those eyes."

The way he looks at me right now—I don't think he means it like a come-on or anything. His gaze is intent, searching my face so obviously, it makes me uncomfortable.

"I don't know what you mean."

"Everyone else here is riding extremes. You're distant but you always look like you're thinking. You keep wandering off alone, which is actually kind of stupid . . . so I just wanted to know what's going on."

"Nothing."

He hesitates. "Where's your family, Sloane?"

"Dead like yours?"

I have no idea if Rhys's family is dead or not until I see how the question cuts him. He winces, but maybe he shouldn't have asked if he didn't want me to rip his chest wide open. He brings his hand to it, palm against it, like he's trying to keep his heart inside. It's like I took something away from him but I don't know what. There's nothing left to take.

"I've never said my family was dead," he says. "What gives you the right?"

He turns and makes his way down the hall before I can answer. I have no choice but to follow him and for some reason, that makes me angry.

"I've always been quiet," I say at his back. "It's not like you knew me before."

He stops and turns. "You're Sloane Price. Your locker is on the diagonal from mine. You and your sister were attached at the hip when she went here, like it was you two and no one else, and I always thought that was weird but I also thought it was kind of sweet. And what you just said to me about my family was really cold."

"So where are they, then? If they're not dead?"

He gives me the dirtiest look and stalks off.

I want to ask him if he's glad we made it but by then he's already gone.

Thud. Thud. Thud. Thud. Thud.

It hasn't stopped. It drives Cary and Rhys into the halls, or maybe they're checking the other doors, I don't know.

Harrison has pieces of wet toilet paper jammed in his ears and he took a bunch of Benadryl we found in the nurse's office, so he's out. We also found blankets and pillows in there so now our mats look like sorry imitations of beds and they feel like them too. I lay on mine and watch the door. I pick a scab clean off my elbow. A blot of blood appears.

I swear the thudding picks up.

Thudthudthudthud.

I pull the blanket up to my chin and I close my eyes. Rhys and Trace settle in on either side of me. Rhys says prayers under his breath and it's the sound I fall asleep to.

Sloane.

I open my eyes and it's minutes later. No, hours. I can't think around the sharp edge of my father's voice in my ears.

A shadow floats across the room and I panic—*he got in, no he didn't, he couldn't have*—when I realize it's Grace and Trace, sneaking out of the auditorium. I squeeze my eyes shut and try to force my dad out of my head but once he's there, he's there.

I decide to follow them.

I leave the auditorium quietly, listening for their voices as I step into the hall. I circle the first floor twice because the building is confusing in the dark, but I don't find them. I move on to the second floor, pausing outside of classroom doors, listening.

A beam of light down the hall catches my eye. The AV room. I hide behind a row of lockers and watch Trace pick through Principal LaVallee's keys while Grace holds the flashlight over his hands.

"Does Cary know you took those?" she asks.

"They're not his keys." Pause. "No."

He finds the right key and opens the door. They hesitate on the threshold. When we were out there stepping into any room, through any doorway, it was like having fear injected right in your heart. It was dangerous. After a long moment, they go in. I move as close to the door as I can and I hear them shuffling around for a while, silent, and then—

"Ready?" Trace.

"They won't be able to see our faces."

"They might. We'll say our names."

Silence.

"I don't want to do this."

"Grace, come on. They knew we were coming to the school."

"But—"

"And I didn't see them die and you didn't see them die, so what if they're trying to get to us? What if we have to leave or what if—what if we die before they get here? If we die before they get here, they'll find this. And if we don't die we can watch it and laugh about it later."

I peer around the door. They're sitting on Ms. Yee's desk, facing a digital camcorder mounted on a tripod in front of them. Grace holds the flashlight under their faces. It makes them look awful. The open LCD screen is glowing, flickering as they move. I sit on the floor and listen. I have no right to this moment but I'm going to take it anyway.

"What am I supposed to say?"

"Whatever's in your heart."

"Trace, come on."

"Do it for me."

"I don't like you talking like we're going to die. You think I'd let anything happen to you? You really think I'd let you die?" It's quiet for a moment and then the sound of Grace's muffled crying drifts into the hall and I risk another look. Trace is holding her now but even so, she's still the one comforting him. "I would never let anything happen to you."

The worst kind of emptiness fills me. Imagine loving someone that much, but imagine them loving you back. I thought I knew what that was like but I didn't. I never did. She lets him go and wipes her eyes. Trace moves from the desk to the camcorder and hits the record button. I stop watching but I stay against the wall and listen.

"My name is Trace Casper and this is my sister, Grace. We're seventeen . . ."

Seventeen and live in Cortege, have lived here all their lives, and attend Cortege High. They're twins. Birth date: March eleventh . . . I fade out until it gets more personal.

"Our parents are Troy and Leanne Casper and if they're still alive, this is for them." Trace clears his throat. "Grace, say something before the battery dies . . ."

"We tried to get to you," she says, and then Trace chimes in, *yes, yes, we tried to get to you,* and suddenly they're both talking over each other. It all comes pouring out.

They talk about how we got to the school and how Trace hates Cary and how the dead are outside the doors and it's the same thudding over and over and how it makes hours feel like days and if the barricades are breached, we have an escape plan but no one knows where we're going next but as soon as they do, they'll put it on the tape so the Caspers know too.

There is this awful moment as they try to describe their state of mind. How do you say that physically, you're okay, when everything is not. They're determined to make it clear that they're scared and sad and lonely and missing their parents while trying to pretend they aren't suffering for it when it's so obvious they are. The closing message is all *I love you*s and just before Trace turns the camcorder off, Grace blurts out, "We're sorry we left you," and then she starts to cry again and I think it isn't enough to survive for the sake of surviving. There has to be more to it than just that. Trace and Grace have each other. This is what they're here for. Why they're still here. Surviving should mean something like it means something to them. And if it doesn't—

If it doesn't.

"Do you think I killed them?"

It's dusk. Cary and I walk down the dimly lit hallway together. Soon it will be dark. When we reach the fork, I'll go to the gym and he'll head to the library to make sure everything's the same as it was yesterday and the day before that. The constant thudding is wearing on me, like a permanent headache behind my eyes. Talking about the Caspers feels the same way.

Because, of course, Cary wants to talk about the Caspers.

"The Caspers?" I ask. He nods, slowing his pace. "What does it matter?"

"Rhys is on my side. Harrison will say whatever he thinks whoever he's talking to wants to hear. I know how Grace and Trace feel. I want to know if you think I killed them."

"They were swarmed. That's what killed them."

"You think it's my fault?"

I stop. Cary stops.

"I think it could have happened to anyone."

He gives me a pained look. "You should be a politician, Sloane."

I pause. I don't think it's his fault but . . .

"You won't repeat it?"

"Never."

"I don't think it's your fault. I don't think you killed them. I think . . ." I shrug. "I think you're crazy good at this survival stuff."

His shoulders sag. He gives me a small, relieved smile and we start walking again, his step a little lighter than it was before. It feels strange to have that kind of power over someone.

"I mean, you're crazy good at it for a stoner who couldn't seem to get his shit together academically at all," I add.

He laughs. "First of all, I only sold. Second, high school was only that thing I was doing until I infiltrated the family business."

"Yay nepotism," I say. He gives me a thumbs-up. His

parents run a small press. I wonder where they were when this started. "Where are your parents, anyway?"

"Toronto. They might have been in the air when it started. Maybe they didn't make it." He says it so easily. He glances at me. "I mean, I just have to think I'm never going to see them, either way. Not hope for anything. Seems greedy to make it this far and want more."

"Does it?"

"Kind of. Do you think Lily made it?"

Hearing someone else say her name makes me want to find something I can crush into dust. Do I think Lily made it. Of course she made it.

"I mean, I'm sure she did," he says hastily.

"You think?"

"She knows how to take care of herself."

"Did you have sex with my sister?"

"Oh, man, Sloane."

"She bought pot from you," I say, and then I keep pushing it because for some reason, I have to know. It's important now. "Did she pay you or . . . ?"

"Yeah, she paid me." Pause. "And we fooled around. Sorry."

I don't know what to say. I'm not shocked or anything, I just don't know what to say. It's something Lily would do. It's something Cary would do. Lily never had a boyfriend when she lived at home, ever. She said it would be too complicated and she'd spin stories about what would happen if an imaginary significant other found out about what our father did to us. The stories always ended in separation—us being ripped from each other. *Never tell.*

For me, that meant never having anyone because she was sure I'd blurt out our secrets to the first person who was nice to me. For her, it meant nobody was allowed to get too close. There were boys who were friends and make-out sessions she'd spill about if she felt like it, but Lily wasn't the Popular Girl. Guys didn't *have* to have her. She was blond and pretty, but mostly she looked tired all the time.

"Fooled around as in had sex."

"Yeah, that would be—yeah." Cary's face turns red. "Wow. Seriously, Sloane. If I just made shit awkward between us, I'm sorry."

"It's okay. It doesn't make things awkward."

"Good."

But then I change my mind. Maybe it's not okay. He fooled around with my sister and sold her drugs and he never looked at me twice before. I don't know why but that bothers me.

"She made it," Cary decides in a voice that tells me he's thinking about being with her, touching her. I feel nauseous. "We were hanging out the night before she left and I knew she'd make it then. I know it now. She's a fighter."

I freeze. There are so many things wrong with what just came out of his mouth.

He was hanging out with her the night before she left.

He knew she was leaving.

"You saw her before she left?"

"Yeah."

"Did she say where she was going?"

He stops as the question settles in.

"No," he says.

I bite my tongue for a full minute. I should leave it at this because it's only going to feel worse if I don't. I should, but I can't.

"Did she say why she was going?"

I know the answer to this, but I want to know if Cary knows. I want to know if whenever they fooled around, she told him about what it was really like in our house.

"No," he says again, softer this time. "Shit, Sloane. I thought you knew. The way you two were . . . I would've never . . ."

"It doesn't make a difference now," I say.

"No," he says. "I guess not."

In the gym, I stare at the doors. My pulse keeps time with each thud, beating hard, filling me with the kind of anger I never thought I could be capable of. I study the desks and step forward. I kick one lightly and then I kick it again, harder. The feel of my shoe against the desk's metal leg is satisfying and sends a little electric jolt through me so I kick it again and again and again until my heart is louder than the thudding. I make a mountain of desks shift just enough that one of them tumbles onto its side. A loud crash fills the gym and breaks me out of my trance. The anger disappears—I don't know where it goes—and I realize what I've done.

I rush at the desk and pull it upright, like the doors are seconds away from bursting open, but they're not. The sound causes a fit outside, though. It makes the dead frantic. Next thing I know, everyone runs into the gym because everyone heard. Cary, Harrison, Rhys, Grace, and Trace. They all ask the same questions.

What's going on, what was that, are they inside, did they get in.

I tell them I don't know what happened, the barricade just moved.

They believe me.

A whole day passes where barely anyone speaks.

Trace does his laps. We eat breakfast, lunch, and dinner to the soundtrack of our impending death. Everyone drifts around the auditorium looking hollowed out. There are dark circles under their eyes. They pace the room stiffly, like they're hundreds of years old. Cary sits against the wall facing the doors and just stares at them. I think the thudding might drive us insane before the doors actually give. Trace thinks we should move to the library—it's quiet there, after all—but no one is willing to do it and that's when he and Cary have the only exchange of the day: Cary says a watched pot never boils. Trace reminds him there are three other doors in here no one is watching. That's when I leave. I circle the first floor for a while, listening as the noise outside the front entrance gets louder and fainter the closer and farther I am from it.

The light wanes.

I walk the same path over and over until I need to stop. I'm not ready to go back to the auditorium, so I end up in the administration office. I push buttons on Mrs. Ramos's computer and watch nothing happen.

I e-mailed Lily after she left, every day for the first two weeks. *How could you do this to me? Who are you?* I know she got them because eventually, they started bouncing back. Account closed. I push the power buttons on the monitor and the tower again. Turn on, turn on. They don't. Carrier pigeons will come back in vogue. My eyes travel over the photos lining the desk. In them, Mrs. Ramos looks happy.

Nothing matters anymore.

The ferocity of this thought makes me want to run back to the gym and shake everyone until their necks snap. Nothing matters anymore. Nothing. My blood goes white-hot and I give the monitor a push without thinking. Not off the desk, just into the wall. It's unsatisfying.

Cary knew she was leaving.

Not thinking about it. I am not thinking about it. I leave the office, closing the door behind me. It clicks shut. The hall is empty, looks kind of burned out in the dark. My gaze moves from the path back to the auditorium, which I'm not ready to go back to, and the stairwell. I climb the stairs to the second floor. When I reach the top of the landing my body feels impossibly heavy like the weight of the sky is on top of me. I make it halfway down the hall before I'm sitting, resting my head against my knees because Cary knew.

He knew.

This is how I imagined it over and over: it's my eighteenth birthday. I wake up before I have to be awake. My bags are next to the door. Seeing them makes my palms tingle, I'm so nervous/excited/scared/excited/nervous/excited. I hear Lily in the hall and all I can think is how lucky I am, how she's the best sister ever. She stayed two extra years just for me so we could leave at the same time, so I wouldn't have to be alone with him. I wouldn't have to be alone. *You'd die without me.* She said it all the time. She said it because it was true. It wasn't a secret.

I'd die without her and she left anyway.

And Cary knew.

I never thought anything could feel like the morning I woke up and she was gone but this is what that feels like. It feels exactly like that. I stretch out on the floor and press my face against the cool tiles. I wait for my blood to turn to cement, for my heart to stop beating. I stay still until everything I'm feeling closes my eyes and the next time they're open a hand is on my shoulder. Rhys is crouched in front of me. I sit up faster than he can stop touching me and he overbalances and nearly falls over. He recovers and then he's looking at me, equal parts concerned and wary. I get to my feet. He does the same. He has a flashlight with him.

"Grace noticed it's been over an hour since you left the auditorium," he says. "I didn't think anything bad happened to you, but . . ."

"The noise is less—" I gesture feebly. "Up here."

As far as explanations go, it's a good one, but still, he chastises me.

"We should stay close together," he says. "You know that."

I nod and rub my face. Brush my hair out of my eyes. I keep doing it and he just stands there and watches until I say, "You can go back. I'll be there soon."

"Did you completely miss the part where I said we should stay close together?"

"I know but," I say, and I stop because I don't know how to finish.

I feel like there are bugs under my skin.

"What's wrong, Sloane?"

"Nothing."

"Yeah, you're really acting that way."

"Okay, everything's wrong."

"Now you're sounding more reasonable."

"It's just—this is . . . it's all . . ."

"It's bad," he finishes. I nod. "I get that but I feel like it's more with you."

A weird sort of laugh flutters past my lips, something bordering on hysteria. He doesn't back away but waits for me to explain, to fill the silence. That's such a dick thing for him to make me do.

"I'm tired, that's all."

"Everyone is."

No, we're not all tired, I want to say. Not like this.

"At night," he says, "I wake up every five minutes thinking I'm at home. It's like I can't get this through my head no matter what." He pauses. "Do you want to go back now?"

Before I can answer, the world explodes.

It's a sound like a bomb going off. I don't know if I felt it first before I heard it or if I heard it first and then I felt it. But I couldn't have felt it. It magnetizes me and Rhys. We reach for each other and he pulls me down the hall as fast as he can and a thrill courses through me. *They got in.* We reach the landing at the same time Cary, Trace, Harrison, and Grace do. Their flashlight glares in our faces. I hold my free hand up to cover my eyes. They're coming up and we're going down.

"It's outside." Cary gasps. "I need to see—we have to know how close it was—we think it might—we think it might be—"

"It's *help!*" Harrison bursts out. He pushes past Cary and Rhys and runs toward the window. Cary screams *"Wait!"* and tears after him and then after a stunned moment, *we* run after Cary, down one hallway and up the next and it's dark because of the poster board over the window but I still make out a lumpy shape beneath it. Cary is holding Harrison, half-restraining him, half really holding him.

"Stop, Harrison, just stop—"

"But they won't know we're here—"

"We can't draw attention to ourselves," Cary says. "We have to think how we're going to do this—we can't just uncover the window, you *know* that—"

"But they're going to leave us—"

"Jesus, you're such an asshole—get off him!" Trace shouts. "All you have to do is take the poster board down and look outside—"

"*Slowly,*" Rhys interrupts. "We have to do it slowly—"

"Then fucking *do it* already!"

We surround the window and pull at the tape holding the poster board up. Cary says *careful* over and over while we're doing it, but no one's careful. Everyone is fevered with the idea of rescue. When the last of the tape releases, the poster board slides to the floor. We jump back and then stand there, terrified of what has to be done next.

Maybe we don't want to see what made that noise after all.

"Someone has to look," Harrison says, but he doesn't move.

No one does for the longest time. Trace finally steps up. He stands in front of the window and leans forward, squinting.

"What is that . . . ?"

We move in next to him so we can see what he's seeing. An intense orange glow lights up the distance. Smoke billows into the night sky.

Fire.

I've only seen something like this once before when

Cortege's old feed mill burned down and the whole town left their beds in the middle of the night to watch the piece of local history get devoured by the flames.

"Where is that?" Grace asks. "Is it close?"

"I think it's Russo's," Cary says. Russo's Gas Station. "Shit . . ."

I let my eyes travel from the fire to the street below. Cortege is almost a parody of itself. Shadows move across the street, the illusion of a former life. Men and women stand in the school's parking lot, the road, before hurrying away, like they have somewhere very important to be. They're all moving that way. All in the same . . .

"God," I whisper.

"What?" Grace asks.

I blink, try to make sure of what I'm seeing.

"They're leaving."

"*What?*"

Waves of dead are running to the fire. Of course. Of course they'd want to investigate, in case there's something there to satisfy their hunger. Other survivors . . .

I want to tell them we're in here.

Grace laughs in disbelief as the school parking lot clears.

"Oh my God . . . they *are*—they're going—they're going away—Trace, they're going away!"

The announcement is slow to sink in but when it does, it really does. Rhys and Cary grin at each other like idiots and Harrison keeps asking, *that's good, right?* I know he knows it's good but he needs to hear someone else say it because it's not real for him until someone else says it.

Trace punches him in the arm and goes *of course it's fucking good!* Everyone is so happy. I turn back to the window and push my hands against the glass.

When we get back to the auditorium, the thudding has stopped.

"—Soon. This is not a test—"

"Blow. Me. Tina T."

Trace says each word loudly into the radio speakers. I push my breakfast away.

Today we're having juice over cereal.

"Tina T?" Harrison asks. "Is that her name?"

"It's what I'm calling her," Trace says over Tina T's voice. "This Is Not a Test."

"Would you turn it off?" Grace asks. "Please?"

He turns it off. Today is subdued, relaxed. Something that could pass for good, I guess.

Everyone is *so glad* the gas station exploded.

"I can't remember the last time I ate breakfast," Grace says, finishing hers.

"How about yesterday?" Trace reminds her. "And the day before and the day—"

"I meant *before* all this started."

"Really?" Rhys asks, but the way he asks isn't like he's actually interested. More like there's a conversation happening and he might as well participate because there's nothing better to do. "It doesn't take that long to eat."

"It does when you're—"

"Student government president," Trace finishes. "An hour and a half in the bathroom every morning, just to get ready for school."

Harrison stares at her. "Why would you do that to yourself?"

"She's got this convoluted makeup routine," Trace says. "Like, every inch of her face had to be covered in product before she was ready to face most of you douchebags."

"*One* of us should care about our appearance."

"You're just insecure because I'm the better looking twin."

The affection Trace has for his sister makes his voice sound like honey to me. The way he teases her makes her eyes light up in a way I haven't seen anyone else's light up since we got here and in a way no one else's will. He notices me staring and my mouth does something it can't help—it smiles at him. He gives me a small smile back.

Rhys yawns.

"Tired?" Cary asks.

"Had a hard time getting to sleep last night. Almost too quiet."

"Don't jinx it," Harrison says.

"*I'm* jinxing it. Seems like there's jack all to worry about today." Trace gets to his feet and stands in front of Cary with his hand out. "Gimme LaVallee's keys. I want to go exploring."

Cary's hand goes to his pocket protectively and he tries to pull a face like he's doing anything but intending to keep them from Trace. "I don't think—"

"I don't give a fuck what you think. Keys. Now."

"He has as much right to them as you do," Grace says before Cary can protest. Her voice is soft but her eyes meet his and they're steel, daring him to disagree. Cary sighs and takes the keys out of his pocket. Throws them at Trace.

"If you happen to see anything useful lying around, feel free to bring it—"

"Get one of your two bitch boys to scavenge for you, Chen." Trace points at Rhys and Harrison. "Because I'm not."

"Oh, fuck off," Rhys says.

Trace flips everyone off and leaves. Cary sits there, cracking his knuckles. I can tell he wants to bitch about what an utter asshole Trace is and how much he'd like to punch him, break his teeth, whatever, but Grace's presence keeps him from doing it. He glances at her a few times.

"You know, just because we've had *one* good night doesn't mean it's time to dick around. I saw a pair of bolt cutters in the custodian's office. We should do a locker raid."

"Sure," Rhys says.

They get to their feet. Harrison gives them a five-second head start before running after them and then Cary turns back to me and Grace.

"Coming?"

I want to, but Grace shudders and shakes her head.

"That's like grave-robbing."

"Sloane?"

Grace looks at me. I get the feeling she wants me to stay.

"I'll pass," I say.

And then it's just Grace and me and it's quiet. She doesn't talk at all and after about ten minutes I'm annoyed I stayed. I guess she doesn't have to speak to me. It's probably not high on her list of priorities. She's got Trace.

"Sloane?"

"Yeah?" I cringe at how eager I sound.

"Will you come to my locker with me? I left my purse in there before everything happened and I want it but I . . ." she laughs, self-conscious. "I don't want to go alone."

"Sure."

Grace's locker is on the first floor, close to the administration office. We walk there wordlessly. Cary's, Rhys's, and Harrison's voices drift back to us from somewhere nearby, but it's hard to tell what they're saying. It sounds effortless though. I hang back at her locker when we get there, unsure of what to do while she thumbs at her combination, straining to see in the poor light. After it's unlocked, she stands in front of the door like she's afraid of it. It's a while before she opens it and when she does, I glimpse cutouts of actors and musicians taped to the door and I wonder what they're doing now, if they're dead. I wonder if they've saved all the celebrities. When this is over, society will need entertainment to get past it. We'll make movies about it, hundreds of movies, and in every one of them, we'll be the heroes and the love interests and best friends and winners and we'll watch these movies until we are so far removed from our own history, we'll forget how it really felt to be here.

Grace grabs her purse. It's a designer purse. I watch her unzip it and riffle through it until she finds what she's looking for. As soon as she does, the purse slips from her grasp and hits the floor. Clutched tightly in her fingers is a piece of paper. She unfolds it and then presses it against her face, breathes it in.

"Look at this," she says. She kisses the note once before she gives it to me. As soon as my fingers curl around it, she says, "Be careful—"

I stare at the bubbly handwriting.

Daughter dear, I didn't manage to throw something together for your lunch—I'm a flake! Here's some money instead. Buy something healthy! Remember, Miss President, the student body looks to you to set a good example!
Love you, xo Mom

The first thing I think is, *Mrs. Casper still makes Grace's lunch?* And then I cross that thought out until it's not even there anymore because it's the kind of thing Mrs. Casper would do and besides—it's a note from Grace's mom. This is what has value. This is the new money.

"Lucky," I say.

"I know. I knew it was here . . . but I couldn't—I mean I just couldn't. Until now," she says. "I just woke up and I really wanted it today. I miss her."

She takes the note back and runs her thumb over it. My throat is so tight and there's a weight in my chest that's hard to breathe around. Memories of my mother are hazy things. They feel like a kid's blanket, fuzzy and soft but mostly insubstantial. Grace's note doesn't make me wish for a woman I spent most of my life not having. It's not that . . .

She looks at me. "Are you okay?"

"I'm fine."

Neither of us moves or says anything for a long time. It's like—suspended animation. I don't know. We could stand here for hours and not say or do anything because there's nothing to say or do. Grace looks at her note and I cross my arms, once again fighting the urge to ask her if she remembers the sleepover. I don't know why I want to but I won't let myself do it.

"Hey!" We turn. Trace makes his way down the hall, twirling LaVallee's keys around his fingers like they're a trophy. Grace picks up her purse, hastily shoving the note inside it. He grins. "I want to show you guys something cool."

We end up in the teachers' lounge.

Cary, Rhys, and Harrison come with us after piling a bunch of their locker finds in the auditorium. Their company makes Trace pissy but as Cary points out, Trace doesn't own the school. They're still bickering when we step into the room. It's on the second floor. The big joke is—was—all the money went here. The lounge has a fridge and flowers (tacky fake bouquets, but still, it's a splash of color), soft couches, chairs, and nice lamps. Storage cupboards and desks. A microwave, a water cooler. Magazines.

"Check this out." Trace rummages in one of the cupboards and when he faces us, he's holding a generous bottle of whiskey. "The rumors are true. I knew they kept good shit in here."

"Alcohol?" Harrison asks, and like that, I can tell he's never drank anything, let alone been drunk before. "Holy shit."

"What's that doing in here?" Rhys asks.

Trace sets the bottle on the table in front of the couches and flicks a tag wrapped around its neck. "Read that. There was an ice-cream cake in the fridge, but it melted."

Grace peers at the tag. "Enjoy your retirement, Vick. We wish we were you."

Vick Bergstein. Our graying world history teacher.

"Think he's enjoying his retirement?" Trace asks, and I laugh before I can stop myself. He soaks it up. "I know, right? He's probably dead. And then I got thinking about the teachers here that I wished were dead, like over and over—like Mrs. Good—and it's funny because now they probably *are* dead and it's like—like that's what I—"

His eyes go wide, almost like he's thinking to himself *I wanted this. I wanted them dead and now it's happened because I wanted it.*

"They weren't all bad, though," Grace says. "I liked Mr. Ford. And Mrs. Lafferty. Mrs. Tipton was kick-ass. I bet she survived. Some of them were great at what they did . . ."

My head is full of faces, faculty members, and I wonder where they are now and if it's a given, like Trace said, that they're all dead. I wonder if I ever wished them dead—if something as simple as that would be the reason I'm here and they're not. But then I think they must've wished *us* dead at some point. They must have. What teacher wouldn't?

Trace stares at the bottle. "So do we open this because we're still alive or do we open it when we're sure we're going to die?"

"We're not going to die," Cary says.

"Didn't you say the same thing to my parents before you sent them in that alley?"

"Give it a rest, Trace."

"Oh, did I hurt your feelings, murderer?"

"They offered to go down that alley first," I say, because for some dumb reason I think that will *help*. But then everyone stares at me and I wish I could put the words back in my mouth. Trace looks like I've gutted him.

"No one asked you, Sloane," Grace says. "And Cary told them it was clear."

"But they offered to do it." My voice gets small. "Cary didn't force them."

"You know what? I'm fucking tired of all of you," Trace declares abruptly, but his voice cracks and I think he's going to cry because he leaves the room with his head down.

Because of me.

How to salvage a moment: Rhys suggests we move whatever we can from the teachers' lounge to the auditorium to make it more livable. No one talks as we fight the couches down the stairs and position them in the corner of the room. We find a lone lunch table we missed for the barricade under the stage, set it up, and steal chairs from the main offices for it. Grace uses the fake bouquets as centerpieces. I feel so sick watching her. I have to make things right. I walk over to her. She fiddles with the flowers. I stand there and try to think of what to say while she ignores me.

"I didn't mean anything by it, just that Cary wouldn't send them there to die," I tell her. "You know he wouldn't."

She looks at me and she's so student government president. Her posture is diplomatic but her tone is frosty. "But he did . . . and they did."

"But—"

"Look, it's hard enough for Trace right now," she says. "If it's how you feel, fine. But I want you to stay away from my brother if you can't keep it to yourself."

She walks away. At first I think I'll cry, but I don't. I'm too jealous of the way she guards Trace to cry and I hate that she thinks of me as someone she has to protect him from.

Eventually, Cary calls us over to the stage. He shows us the locker haul. They found toothpaste—we take turns passing the tube around and dabbing microscopic globs on our fingers—floss, deodorant . . . there are some clothes, which makes Grace happy. I spot a pink sweater with a name written on the tag: CORRINE M. Corrine Matthews.

I remember her curly black hair and smile and then I don't want to touch it.

There's lots of candy and gum. Some lighters and cigarettes. I look at Rhys, expecting him to be happy about it but he doesn't look happy about it

We settle in for the night. The room is . . . the word *home* crosses my mind, but it's not the right one to use. Lily and I used to play house. I was eight, she was ten, and Mom was dead, but Mom had been dead for a while by then, so I guess that's not an important part of this memory. I had dolls and an old box. She had paper, pencils, and erasers and she'd ask questions while I leaned Barbie up against a flimsy cardboard wall and tried to figure out what to do with Ken.

How big should the bedrooms be? Should we have a guest bedroom? Okay. Separate bathrooms for sure. No, Dad doesn't need a room, Sloane. Because he's not going to live with us. This is our house.

"*Grace! GRACE!* Dad's alive! He's outside! *He's ALIVE!*"

Trace bursts into the auditorium screaming these words at the top of his lungs and then we're awake like we were never asleep.

Mr. Casper. Alive.

Trace is breathless and crying as he leads us to the second floor. The flashlight jerks in his hands as he tries to explain. "I couldn't sleep—I was wandering around and I heard him, he was calling for help—I went to the window and I saw—"

Mr. Casper. He's alive, in the parking lot, calling for help.

Rhys is going *are you sure? Are you sure you're sure? Maybe you were sleepwalking.* Trace is so beside himself he doesn't even tell Rhys to fuck off.

We sprint down the halls and up the stairs so fast my lungs feel like they're going to explode. My heart is numb. I don't believe this. I can't believe in this.

Mr. Casper is alive.

"I told you, Grace, I told you—they knew we were here—I knew one of them would try to get to us—I fucking *knew it*!"

I'm at the window first. Trace hands the flashlight to Harrison and pushes himself against me, forces me into the glass. We look past the edge of the auditorium roof, trying to see, searching—Mr. Casper, *alive*—but the lot is empty. Dawn edges up the horizon, but it's not doing it fast enough. It's not light enough to see anyone or anything.

"Where?" Rhys asks. "I don't see him—"

"He was . . ." Trace nudges us away. "He—"

"How could you even see—"

"Shut up—"

"Listen," Cary hisses. "Just listen."

I press the side of my head against the glass and listen with everything I have. I hear car alarms in the distance. Grace takes a sharp breath in.

Trace spins around. "What—"

She points and I follow her outstretched finger to the

crumpled shape of a man facedown on the pavement. I don't know how we missed it at first, until I realize we missed it because we were looking for signs of life.

"No—no," Trace says. "No—that's not—he was alive—"

I squint. It could be anyone from here. I don't know how Trace could have made out his father's face in this lack of light. I'm too afraid to ask him in front of Grace.

"If he's dead, infected can't be far off," Cary says. "Was he shouting?"

"He's not dead! He was standing—he was up! He's just hurt or something—he just—*Dad!* We have to go out—we have to bring him back in—we have to help—"

"Trace—"

I tune them out. The parking lot is empty. I look for others—the shambling, broken bodies of people we used to know surrounding the school again—but there's nothing.

"Dad! *DAD!*"

Cary pulls Trace away from the window but Trace is made of the kind of energy people with hope have. He frees himself and shoves Cary against a row of lockers.

"Don't fucking touch me—"

"You don't even know it's him—"

I hear it first and then I see it: Trace drives his fist into Cary's face. It's a dull sound, but I know it's a sharp hurt. I know what it feels like. Cary's knees buckle but he doesn't fall. He rights himself and stands there, stunned, while blood trickles from his nostrils. He brings his hand to his face and stares at his stained fingertips and I see his anger building in a way I'm not sure anyone else can. It's from his heart, in his veins. I almost want to tell everyone to back away but I watch, transfixed, instead.

"You're useless—" Trace spits at him. "You fucking *murderer!*"

Cary tackles Trace and they're a sloppy mess of fists and legs and Grace is screaming *get off him, get off my brother!*

Rhys is the one who separates them. He has to hold Trace down in the end by climbing on top of him and pushing his knee into Trace's back.

I turn back to the window, the man outside.

Trace gasps under Rhys. "We're wasting time—"

"He's *not moving,* Trace—"

"Are you sure it's him?" I ask.

"Who else would it be? I have to go out there—I have to get him—"

"*No!*" Grace says. "You are *not* going out there. You can't—" And Trace says, *Grace, it's Dad, I know it is, I saw him, we have to get him* because he believes this. He's fevered with it. It's his father out there because it can be no one else.

And she's saying, "No, you *can't.* You can't leave me—"

She repeats this over his insistence he has to go outside and the more she says it, it's like the more she believes he will leave her until she's crying so hard she's hyperventilating. Trace tries to reach for her, but he can't unless Rhys gets off him. When Rhys does, Trace holds Grace and she sobs all over his shirt. He holds her and stares at me, at the window beyond me, trying to soothe her and figure this out at the same time. Then his eyes spark. He turns to Cary.

"You go out there and get him."

Cary stares. "*What?*"

"It's your fault he's out there. Go out there and bring him back in."

"Go out there yourself—"

"I'm not leaving Grace," Trace says. "This is your fault, so you do it."

"I am *not* dying for you," Cary says through his teeth. "And fuck you for asking me—that guy out there? Whoever he is? He's *dead*."

Cary storms down the hall. It must be awful to find out your life is worth nothing to someone else. I want to tell Cary he's not worthless. Harrison probably needs him. Rhys stares at Trace, disgusted, but Trace doesn't care. He closes his eyes and leans his cheek against Grace's head. He has no other options.

"Grace, I have to do it."

"No. *No.*"

He breathes in and tightens his grip on her.

"It's him. I know it is."

I get that feeling again. That ache to have what Trace and Grace have, along with the sharp reminder that I don't. The parking lot is still empty save for the man on the ground. Trace's words echo in my head *we have to bring him back in* and I don't know why they do until it hits me and I finally understand them for what they really are: an out.

"I'll do it," I hear myself saying. "I'll go."

I stop at my locker for my letter to Lily and tuck it carefully in my pocket. I have this insane fantasy where my sister comes across my body on the ground or walking around and she finds the note on me and reads the note and it kills her.

When I get to the library, Cary is actually helping Trace with the door, which is unreal to me. Blood is crusted under Cary's nose. Trace is shaky, vibrating with the possibility of his father being out there, dead or alive. I watch him closely, looking for some indication he knows it can't really be Mr. Casper. There are none. His heart will hold on to it until he knows for sure.

Grace and Harrison sit on one of the tables together. Harrison keeps the flashlight trained on the boys and says he's afraid of the door being open for the brief second it will take me to walk out of it but no one comforts him. Grace is zoned out, like she can't really understand how this happened or why but I can tell she wants me to go out there. I know she does.

"You don't have to do this," Rhys says.

"Shut up." Trace grunts as he pushes a desk aside. "She wants to."

I nod. "I want to."

Rhys sighs, resigned, and then he says something terrible.

"I'll go with you." No. No. *No.* I open my mouth to protest but he cuts me off. "I mean, let's just say if by some miracle the guy out there isn't dead—"

"My father is *not* dead," Trace says loudly.

Rhys ignores him. "That means you have to get him back inside and there's no way you're going to be able to do it alone. It's a two-person job. Unless you *want* to die."

Ha ha. My stomach turns. This went from good to bad, just like that, but I can't let it stop me. I work quickly to rationalize it. It's better this way. It makes it easier. Instead of leaving Trace and Grace high and dry, Rhys can go back and tell them if it's Mr. Casper or not. If it's Mr. Casper, Rhys can get him back into the school. And me—when I go,

I won't have that on my conscience. That would be good. It's a good thing that Rhys is coming with me. It's good.

"Fine," I say. "Okay."

Trace and Cary move the last shelf aside, leaving the door naked before us. Rhys bends down and tightens his shoelaces. I do the same.

"Why are you doing this?" He doesn't ask me quietly enough.

"I was wondering too," Grace says. "Is it because of . . ."

She stops but I know what she's going to say. *Is it because of what I said to you?* I don't know how to tell her I'm sorry I hurt her but it's nothing to do with her. I don't think I can. I knot my shoelaces twice and get to my feet. She waits on my answer.

"I like your family." It's the only thing I can think of to say.

Her face softens. I wonder if she's thinking of the sleepover. Something inside me just wants to see her remember it like Trace wants it to be his father outside because—I don't know.

I guess it's the last thing I have.

"Okay," Cary says.

Trace gives me a hug and I lose myself in the sensation. It's so dizzyingly nice, like someone wants me and I almost think it would be worth hanging around for if it was an all-the-time thing. He lets me go, gives Rhys a curt nod, and then hands us each a baseball bat. I hold mine limply at my side. Rhys clutches his so hard his knuckles turn white.

"Stay by the door," he tells Cary. "Don't move and open it when you hear us."

"I'm not moving," Cary says. "Good luck."

Rhys looks at me. His eyes ask if I'm ready. I nod. I'm more ready than there are words for. Cary pushes the door open. It's still dark. A cool April breeze drifts in and curls around us, making me realize how stale the air is in here. I take a gulp of it and hold it in my lungs.

Rhys and I step outside.

The door closes quietly and firmly behind us.

The fence is in front of us. We back into each other automatically, checking both sides. Nothing. There's nothing. I feel Rhys breathing against me, scared out of his mind.

"Do you *really* think it's Mr. Casper?" he whispers.

"I don't know," I say.

"I don't want to die today, Sloane."

We stare down the path that leads to the athletic field. It's a blind spot, totally wide open. We don't know what's out there. The path to the front of the school is gated, slightly closer to the parking lot but it's still a walk around the building. And if the gate is locked, we'll have to climb it. We won't be soundless doing it.

I wouldn't care if Rhys wasn't here but now I have to care. When there's more distance between us, that's when I'll leave, but for now I have to be careful for his sake. I'm not selfish like Lily. I nod in the direction of the front of the school. Rhys swallows and nods back. I make my way forward but he grabs my arm.

"Let me—" his voice cracks. "Let me go first."

I shake my head but he trudges ahead of me anyway. I follow him, glancing over my shoulder repeatedly. We reach the gate. He ducks and I duck beside him.

We press our faces against the chain link and look around.

The street ahead seems empty, looks almost normal, like the world has yet to wake up, but as our eyes adjust to the dark, things that are wrong slowly begin to assert themselves. The windows in the house across the street are all broken and the front door is wide open. I can see a shape that looks like a body on the lawn. There's a car wrapped around a telephone pole and I imagine a man or woman slumped over the steering wheel, killed on impact. That must have been a good way to go. But there's nothing else that we can see.

No dead.

Maybe they're still at Russo's.

Rhys tests the gate. Locked.

"We should go over together," he says.

We stick the toes of our running shoes through the links. The gate rattles under our weight and the baseball bats clang against the metal. Rhys holds his breath. As soon as he clears the top, he jumps. I do the same, landing easily. He grabs my arm again and pulls me behind a pair of decorative hedges at the corner of the front of the school.

"Didn't see anything. Did you?"

I shake my head. We make our way alongside the building, tiptoeing over flowerbeds until we're interrupted by the concrete walk close to the main entrance.

We cling to shadows every time we make a noise we

shouldn't and then move on more quickly than before. We finally get to the opposite corner of the school, past the bike rack, and stand just before the parking lot. Rhys stops suddenly.

"What if he's been bitten?" he asks, and I swear we both have the same thought right after he asks it. *Why didn't anyone think of that before now?*

"He didn't get back up," I say. "He's not bitten."

And then I step into the lot, feeling the bravest and most indestructible I've ever felt in my life which is strange, I guess, because I'm readying myself to die. The morning air is so welcome against my skin.

"Sloane," Rhys says.

I make my way around a car, checking the ignition. No keys. Rhys takes a few more steps and then he stops again and I know he won't go any farther, that I will have to do this part on my own. I keep walking until I'm standing in the middle of the lot and that's where I see him.

It's not Mr. Casper.

I know that right away. I don't know who he is that he got all the way to the school, begged for help, and ended up facedown on the pavement, but he's got blood on him and he's bulky in a way that reminds me of my father.

But it's not my father, either.

I walk over to the body. This isn't part of my plan. I was supposed to keep walking forward but for some reason I want to see even though it's not Mr. Casper and it's not my father.

This man was someone. He's dead but he was alive. Maybe I knew him. Maybe I passed him on the street once. Maybe he has a note in his pocket for someone like I do. I crouch down, grab him by the shoulders, and roll him onto his back. His face is swollen, bruised. I do a quick check for bites just in case, but I don't see any. I don't see anything that would've killed him either. Maybe he survived this long and his heart gave out or something. He's middle-aged. Wispy hair, balding. Lines edge the corners of his eyes and mouth. I wish dying was as easy as lying down next to him and stealing his death from him.

"Sloane, what are you doing?"

"I'm not coming back with you," I say.

"What?"

"Go back and tell them it wasn't Mr. Casper."

"What the hell are you talking about?"

"I'm leaving—" I look up at him. I can't figure out a way to say it. A good enough way to say it. A way that he will understand. "I can't."

"You'll die out here—"

"I know."

His mouth hangs open but his eyes flicker in a way that tells me he gets it. If he gets it all he has to do is go back inside.

But he doesn't.

Before he can say or do anything, the man's eyes open. Rhys pales. *"Shit!"*

I drop my bat. It clatters against the ground, startling the man into awareness. He makes a noise, something halfway between a groan and a wail. He sits up, scrambles to his feet, and pushes me back—I fight to keep my balance—and then he's babbling.

"No, no, no, no—get away from me!"

"It's okay," I say stupidly. I turn back to Rhys and he shakes his head. What do we do now. I don't know what to do now. This wasn't my plan. "It's—"

"*No!*" The man sinks to his knees and then gets up again. "Where's Nick? *Nick?*"

I step after him. "Just—"

"*Get away from me!*"

"It's okay," I repeat. I walk over to him and before I can do anything, he charges at me, shoves me back hard. I land on my elbows and wince. I get to my feet slowly, feeling blood trickle down my arms, and look to Rhys, who is totally paralyzed by this turn of events.

"We can help," I say. "We have shelter—"

"Stay *away*. Where's Nick? Nick? *Nick!*"

The man wanders away from me, farther down the parking lot, and his voice gets louder and louder and louder as he calls for Nick, whoever Nick is. I turn to Rhys.

"Go back, Rhys. Go back inside—"

And then—breathing.

But it's not breathing like the way I breathe or the way Rhys breathes. It's something that is a sick imitation of life.

It's how they give themselves away.

That house on Rushmore Avenue. We heard them first before they broke in. This awful choked, ragged sound that told us to leave as fast as we could. We have trained ourselves to run from it, to fear it.

I look around but I can't source it. I want to know where it's coming from so I can move toward it. It echoes around us, brings Rhys back to himself.

"Forget him—forget about him—we have to go back."
Rhys walks backward as he says it, heading toward the gate.
"Sloane, we have to go back *now*—"

"I'm not going with you," I say.

"*Nick?* Nick . . ."

I have to get this man to shut up. I have to get this man
to shut up for a minute so Rhys can get back. I hurry over
to him, my brain slowly registering other things as I do,
like his shirt is half open. There are holes in the legs of his
pants. There are red splotches all over him. He's twitching
and he whirls around when I'm within reach. He raises his
fist. I flash to my father, stop in my tracks.

"Don't you come closer—don't—"

I call back to Rhys, my eyes on the man. "Get inside
while you can. I'm staying—"

"I'm *not* going back without you."

I turn to him.

This is the moment everything goes wrong.

At least five infected are running for Rhys, coming in
from all directions, stragglers alerted to us by the man's
shouting. They materialize from seemingly nowhere, some
kind of hibernation. I yell for Rhys to get back into the
school but he's a deer in the headlights.

I don't want to die today, Sloane.

I run to him.

"Rhys, go!"

I make it to him first, I get in front of him and the weight
of at least three infected are on me, pushing at me as they
fight for my body. I lose my footing and lurch forward. One
of the dead—a girl—grabs my arm and pulls me to her and

Rhys finally wakes up. He grabs my other arm and pulls me to him but as hard as he pulls, the dead girl pulls harder while the other four scramble around her for a piece. They all want at me. *I'm the prize,* I think stupidly—and then my shoulder pops out of its socket. I scream. Rhys grabs his bat and smashes it against the dead girl's wrists, smashes it into the others, whatever he can do to get me free and I'm thinking about how it'll never work, how this is it, when the dead girl's grip loosens. Rhys grabs my arm, the wrong arm, and the world comes into the cruelest kind of focus, makes me realize something. We can't go back. They'll follow us to the door. And then it's not just Rhys, it's everyone, I'll risk everyone and I'm not Lily, I would never do what she did to me—

"We have to lead them away," I say. "We have to—"

But they'll follow you no matter where you go. My brain puts the puzzle together before I even know what the pieces are and I run into the parking lot, Rhys close behind me, all the dead following fast. My chest aches, my lungs can't hold air. My feet hit the ground so hard I feel it in my bones. We round the parking lot and the man is still there. When he sees us, all of us, his eyes widen. I close the distance easily and—I push him.

The man grabs on to me. We fall and he lands a second after I do and it's a second I have on him. I use my good arm to scramble to my feet. The man reaches for me. I kick him in the—face. I hear myself kick him in the face. His teeth. Rhys is ahead of me now. I run after him because I don't want to be near what is about to happen, what I made happen.

"Help me—help me—"

I look back. I can't help myself.

They're feeding. Four of them. But one—that girl—hasn't lost sight of us yet. She pursues us, her hair flying around her head. She's not wearing a shirt and all of her exposed skin is gray. The veins beneath it are dark, angry lines that want to break free, be outside of her. Her lips twitch, revealing vicious teeth.

"Come on!" Rhys shouts. *"COME ON!"*

We finally reach the athletic field. It's wide open but there are no other infected, none that I can see. I can hear the girl behind me, though, and she's close, she's fast, faster.

She dives for me and we both crash to the ground. The side of my forehead connects with the pavement. I swear I hear it *crack* and then I'm underwater and everything is strange and removed and I'm strange and removed from it. I turn myself over, slowly, painfully, and stare into milky white irises, all the capillaries around them busted and red. I lose focus. I see one of her, two of her, three of her. Calm settles over me. She licks her lips. I close my eyes.

This is it. Finally.

A splintering sound reaches my ears and then again, again and again. Something splitting open. At first I think it's me, that when you die, you splinter into a million pieces, but then I feel wet—wet against me, but slick and wrong. And then a dead wet weight on top of me.

Rhys hooks his arms under my arms and pulls me out from under the girl and I blink and she comes into focus; her head is completely decimated, bits of blood and brain all over me, and then I'm on my feet but I don't feel like

I'm on my feet. Rhys drags me by the hand and I trip after him. Everything is turning gray. He urges me on.

"Come on, you can do this—"

It's quiet around us now but he moves like we're still being chased. My legs are rubber and I fall. I can't breathe. He pulls me up again, wraps his arm around my waist and we both stagger to the library door. He pounds his fists against it and I slump to my knees.

"Open the door—*open the fucking door*!"

PART TWO

Part Two

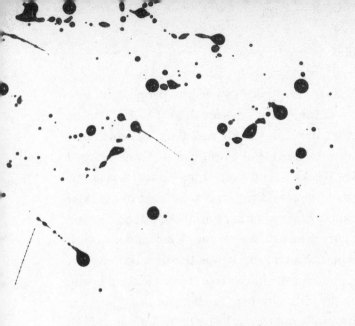

Sometimes I'm brave. Like the sleepover at Grace's. I wasn't supposed to be there. I went without permission but I was willing to face my father's wrath after just so I could have something nice, a memory that belonged only to me. And it was nice. I told Grace I liked her family and she said she noticed me watching her parents a lot and I said I wasn't used to seeing parents together, up close. I guess I could if I watched more TV but that wouldn't be real and when it's real and it's in front of you, two happy people who love each other, a family—that's better than TV. I got to be part of that for a day. Lily was so mad about having to pick up the pieces afterward, but I still did it. I was brave. I tried leaving. Weeks before everything ended, I was one half of Lily's old plan and my bags were next to my door and I don't know how my father found out but he did and he was so angry I had to stay home from school until it didn't show on me anymore. It was the first time he lost control enough to hit me in the face. I tried leaving again, but Lily took the pills with her. Tried again . . .

After Rhys pulls me through the door, I go outside of myself somehow. I don't know how. I wish I knew how. They drag me to the locker room, the showers. Even the shock of freezing cold water against my body can't bring me back. I watch them scramble to get me clean. They keep asking Rhys if I've been bitten, if I'm turning. He says *no* but he also says *wait—be careful—wait until most of the blood's off . . .*

They keep me under the showerhead forever. They keep me under until my lips turn blue and the water runs clear and then Cary sets my shoulder. I come back to myself for this, for how dizzyingly awful it feels, how familiar. My shoulder has been dislocated before. My father. He watched videos on YouTube about how to put everything back in place so we wouldn't have to go to the hospital. So I know what's coming. More pain. I bite down so hard I think my teeth will shatter. Cary tells me *it's okay, it's okay,* but it's not and then it's done, it's over. I close my eyes and the next time I force them open, it's like looking at the world through distorted glass. I don't know where I am at first and then—I remember. The school.

But I don't know where in the school.

My heart beats fast. I touch my forehead. It's been bandaged sloppily. I blink until my vision clears and I process all these things at once: the nurse's office. I am in the nurse's office on a cot with a thin sheet covering me, my forehead is bandaged and I am wearing a scratchy long sweater that isn't mine, that I don't remember changing into. I don't know what is more distressing to me; someone changing my clothes or the hurt. My bones are screaming, my skin feels raw. I try to take some kind of weird comfort in the fact these feelings aren't ones I'm not used to. I've been variations of hurt my whole life. My heart calms. I look around. The door is wide open and the hall is empty. I try to gauge the time. The room is light enough. Day.

I sit up slowly, carefully.

"Still here."

Rhys sits in a chair against the wall, in front of a poster about the dangers of crystal meth. It's a series of photos, the progression of one woman's face over the course of a year on the drug—from haggard to cracked-out. She reminds me of the girl outside and then I get so dizzy with those memories, I feel like I'm going to fall into the sky. I lay back on the cot and take steadying breaths in and out. Rhys walks over and rests his hand against my forehead but there's nothing comforting in his touch and he does it so quickly, I wonder if I imagined it.

"How am I?"

My voice is gravel. He presses a bottle of water into my shaking hands. I drink it and miss my mouth. The water trails down my chin and onto this sweater that's not mine.

Rhys takes the water back from me.

"You're sick." The way he says it, I can't tell if it's an insult or a diagnosis. "Maybe you're concussed. Maybe you have brain damage. But then I think you must have been totally brain damaged before we went out there, so—"

"Rhys—"

"Or *maybe*," he continues, "you're infected. Maybe you'll be dead in hours and then you'll come back—"

"Stop it."

"But you went out there to die, didn't you? So who cares."

I turn my face away from him. He's right. Who cares. Maybe I'm infected. I try to listen to what's happening inside me. If there's any part of me that's dying and becoming something rotten but more purposeful than what I am now.

"You went out there to die, didn't you."

I close my eyes.

"Sloane."

I open them.

"Yes."

He moves away from me like I *am* infected, and then he kicks his chair. Hard. It rattles into the wall and I flinch and he whirls around so fast, my hands automatically fly up to my face. *Don't hit me.* It's such a bad thing to do. He knows I think he'd hurt me and his eyes widen and he steps back.

"You let me go out there with you," he says. "You *risked* my *life*—"

"I wasn't going to let you die—"

"Oh, fuck you, Sloane—"

"I *wasn't*! I didn't—"

"Well, it came just a little too close for my comfort—"

"*You* wouldn't let me go! I wanted to go and you wouldn't let me—"

"If you want to die, do it like a normal person—slit your wrists or something! Jesus!" Too much. I press my fingers into my temples and fight the urge to puke. He grabs pills from the table beside me and holds them out to me. I eye him warily. "It's Tylenol. Just take it."

I take the pills, swallow them dry.

"That man out there," he says. I pick at my blanket. Maybe if I act disinterested enough he'll stop talking. "He's dead because of you. Think he wanted to live?"

"It could've been me," I say. "But you wouldn't go back inside without me."

"Because I couldn't believe what I was hearing—"

"*Why?* Why couldn't you? Have you *seen* it out there, Rhys? There's nothing out there anymore, there's *nothing*—"

"That's such bullshit, Sloane! And even if it wasn't, you don't get to decide that for me—"

"And *you* don't get to decide that for *me*!"

Stalemate. He knows I'm right. He digs his hands into his pockets and tosses a crumpled piece of paper at me and then he leaves. I open it up. It's water-stained, the handwriting mostly melted, save for a few words here and there. My suicide note to Lily.

I'm struggling to stay awake when Grace comes in. I don't want to close my eyes because every time I do I see the man, I see the dead girl, I see Rhys kicking the chair against the wall. But mostly it's the man, staggering around the parking lot calling out for his friend? Lover? Brother? Father? It cuts through me. Did he want to live? Was he fit to live? Was that my call to make? I have to push what I've done all the way to my toes, as far from my head as it can get, otherwise, I'll never be able to let it go. *Murderer.* That's what Grace and Trace call Cary, but it's not Cary, is it. It's me. That's what I'm thinking when I hear Grace's footsteps and then she's standing in the door. She makes a concentrated effort not to look directly at me.

"Rhys said you might not want to see anyone." I'm trying to figure out what else Rhys might have said when she continues. "But I wanted to see you."

I try to guess what's coming next. *He said you went out there to die. He said you're crazy. He said you're a risk to the rest of us. He said you're a murderer.*

"He said the man was hurt. Dying." She pauses. "He said it wasn't my dad."

So he didn't out me.

"It wasn't your dad," I say.

She exhales like now she can believe it. She crosses the room and sits on the edge of my cot. She picks at her fingernails for a while before saying, "I don't understand you."

"What's there to understand?"

"You didn't . . . you didn't do it because of what I said to you, did you? Because you wanted to make it up to me?"

"Does it matter?"

"I didn't want it on me if you'd died."

"I made the choice. It wouldn't have been on you," I say. "Like your parents."

"Shut up."

"They offered to go first."

"Shut up, Sloane."

"We both saw it happen."

"Oh, so you think because you went out there you can say this shit to me," she says, collecting herself. "It doesn't work that way."

I shrug and close my eyes again. I want to sleep. I want her to leave so I can do it. I let myself doze, feel my breathing even out.

After a while, she moves from the cot.

"You know what I hate?" she asks, and I surface enough to ask her. "The way everyone talks about it. How my parents *chose* to go into that alley, like they were aware of the fact they might die. But they wouldn't have done it if they thought there was the remotest chance. No one thinks about that."

"But they did do it," I say.

"Because they thought it was *clear*," she says, and then she pushes my hair away from my face and it's such a tender gesture, it confuses me. It's so at odds with the harshness of the words coming out of her mouth. "There was *no way* they would have gone into that alley first if they thought it was too dangerous because they had *us*. Why do you think they let Cary lead the way that whole time when they were the adults? They did it so if anything happened, he died. *Not* them. They went in that alley because he told them it was clear and he was wrong."

"He's sorry."

"If he was sorry, he would've gone out there tonight. Oh, and Trace wants to thank you." Her voice breaks. She exhales. "I think you made him finally understand that they're dead."

I curl up onto my side and stay as still as possible until she finally leaves and then I breathe so quietly, I can't hear myself. I pretend I'm dead. Eventually everything disappears.

But when it comes back, it comes back as strange, uneven footsteps.

Someone entering the room. A rough, calloused hand against my cheek. It doesn't belong to anyone in this building I can think of. Fingertips trace my face and I think I must still be asleep and dreaming, but I don't want this dream, whatever it is, so I turn my face away from the touch and then the footsteps retreat and I realize I *am* awake. I sit up fast, bleary-eyed, and stare at the open door to the nurse's office. From here, the hall seems empty, seems cold. Was I awake? I get up slowly, my body groaning, and pad out of the office. I stand in the hall, unsure of my next steps. It's dark and I feel exposed and I want to know who touched me because the more awake I get the more awake I'm sure I was when it happened and I can't deny the familiarity of the touch but I need to deny its reality.

I walk past the administration office, guiding myself by

shadows. I stand at the barricades against the front entrance and try to remember what it felt like to come through the doors every day when this was just a school. I can't.

And then my whole body goes rigid.

The charged feeling of another presence in the air. I step forward, my eyes traveling over nothing. I bring my hand to my face and move back down the hall, the way I came, when I get another weird feeling, like I'm being watched. And then a musky scent coats the inside of my throat. My chest tightens. It feels like I'm being wrapped in plastic. I wonder if I'll remember him forever, if nothing will disappear the feel of his hands, his scent.

"Dad," I say.

The hall crackles with my voice, breaking the spell. I fumble back to the nurse's office and sit on the edge of my cot, waiting for the invisible hand that's squeezing my heart to let it go. I grab the flashlight and turn it on its lowest setting and it catches my note to Lily on the table. I unfold it and smooth it out over and over until I calm down.

I wonder if she hears him where she is now, if she hears his voice and his footsteps in her dreams. I wonder if she hears him when she's awake or if she stopped hearing him as soon as she left, if everything got more okay the more distance she put between us. Or maybe the voice and the footsteps she hears are mine. I hope they are. I hope I'm the ghost that belongs to her.

"Ready to join the land of the living?"

I wince. Even Cary cringes as soon as it's out of his mouth.

"I guess," I say.

He brought me clothes from the drama department. A plaid men's shirt and a pair of jeans that don't fit. I look rural. The buttons of the jeans dig uncomfortably into my abdomen. I changed into them in the little bathroom across the room and when I came out, he was still there, waiting to ask me that. Am I ready.

"What's it like out there?" I ask. "I mean . . . outside."

"There are a few stragglers, but they're mostly in the streets. They haven't gone back to the doors, which is good," he tells me. "We covered the windows again, just in case. Do you feel okay? You were pretty out of it when we brought you in here."

The bandage on my head itches. It also looks stupid, but it would be ungrateful to say so. The side of my face is scratched, red. My cheek is bruised. Lots of bruises have exploded all over my body in the last twenty-four hours. I feel like I was in a minor car accident but I tell him I'm fine and he says, "I'll bet," and then we both stand there uncertainly. He stares at me for so long, it makes me prickly and hot.

"What?" I ask.

He shrugs. "I was just surprised you were the one who went out there."

"Everyone was."

"Yeah, but it probably should've been me."

"Why would you even say that?"

"Because that's what Grace and Trace keep telling me. I don't know. Now Trace is saying I almost had your blood on my hands too."

"You wouldn't have."

He exhales slowly. "You mean that?"

"It wasn't about you, Cary."

"What was it about?" I look away from him. And then he says, "Rhys told me."

"Rhys told you what?"

"About the man out there. What you did. Rhys said he was half crazy and that he would've jeopardized us if you brought him in. Now he's—he's one of the stragglers . . ."

So the man turned. My eyes burn. I don't want to talk about it with Cary, though, so I twist the topic back around to Grace and Trace.

"They're in mourning. They just need to get through it . . ."

"*Everyone*'s in mourning," he says. "There's a whole *world* out there to mourn. The only difference between them and us is they got their parents a little longer and the only reason they survived as long as they did was because of *me* and—" He struggles to force the next words out. "I apologized to them and they never once thanked me for getting them this far."

"They're probably not going to."

"Don't worry, I'm not holding my breath."

It's quiet for a minute and then I kind of lie. It's not a bad lie, though. Maybe it will make him feel better. I look him in the eyes and I say, "Thank you."

It doesn't have the desired result. It doesn't make him feel better. Instead, Cary seems to get sadder. He forces a half smile at me, but I see through it.

"Let's go back," he says.

When I get to the auditorium, everyone looks at me and that makes it feel more like high school than anything. Before anyone can speak, Trace crosses the room and hugs me. It hurts. He doesn't speak, just holds me until Rhys finally says, "I went out there too."

"And you got your pat on the back." Trace releases me and when he looks at me, his eyes are all warmth. "Thank you for what you did for us, Sloane."

"Forget it." I want everyone to forget it.

"I want you to know it means something to me that you tried." He looks past me and the warmth disappears from his eyes. "Unlike some people."

"Fuck you," Cary says tiredly.

"Who's got breakfast?" Rhys asks. "I did it yesterday. Not doing it today."

"I do," Trace says.

Surprising. I don't think Trace has gotten breakfast once since we got here, and it's not like there's anything to prepare. Grab packaged food, an assortment of drinks, toss on tray. He jogs over to the stage and hoists himself up, disappearing behind the curtain.

"Kitchen's the other way," Rhys calls. No sooner is it out of his mouth than Trace reappears with—the whiskey. "That's not exactly what I had in mind when I said breakfast."

"Why didn't we get drunk on this the day we found it?" Trace hops offstage. "What exactly are we waiting for again? I don't think we have time to wait on this."

"All we have is time," Grace says.

"Yeah, but who knows how long that is? Fuck tomorrow and the day after and the day after that." He opens the bottle, moves to take a swig, and stops. He holds it out to Rhys and me. "It should be you two first. For what you did."

"You're a douchebag," Cary says.

Trace ignores him and pushes the bottle at us. Rhys takes the whiskey first, brings it to his mouth, and drinks it easily. He hands the bottle to me. I mimic Rhys but unlike him, I nearly choke. It burns all the way down. I hand the bottle back to Trace. He drinks and hands it to Grace, who grudgingly passes it to Cary after she takes her swig. We go in a circle. Harrison has such a hard time with it, he grabs a bottle of juice from the kitchen to cleanse his palate. In that moment, he looks too young to be alive.

"Pussy," Trace says.

Grace elbows him. "Better than wasting it."

And then we realize this is it as far as booze goes, at least. A bottle of whiskey. This is all we have. It's unlikely there will be any more hidden around the school, waiting to be found.

Trace sets the bottle on the floor and we all have this convoluted discussion about how much we should drink, if we should just go for it or if, you know, moderation is the key.

"It should be fair," Cary says.

"Hey, if life was fair, you wouldn't be here," Trace says. Cary doesn't rise to it. I feel so bad for him today. "Also, fun isn't always fair."

"Well, we're not staying sober while you get wasted," Rhys says.

"Now *that's* a good idea," Trace says, but no matter how hard he tries, he can't rouse the rest of us into agreeing with him. I don't know who says *drinking games* first but someone does, and that is how we all end up on the floor playing I Never. Trace seems really satisfied about this turn of events, so maybe he'll have some kind of edge on the rest of us. Maybe he's done everything or maybe he'll just lie and say he has. He starts us off, anyway.

"I have never skinny-dipped in Pearson Lake." An awkward silence follows and Rhys and Cary drink. A ghost of a smile crosses Trace's face. "At the same time?"

"Fuck off." Rhys grabs the bottle from Cary. "I've never cheated on a test."

"Bullshit," Cary says.

"I'm so brilliant, I've never had to."

Everyone drinks except Harrison.

"I have never engaged in sexting," Cary says.

Trace. Rhys. Trace freaks when he sees Grace reach for the bottle.

"With who?" he asks. Grace smiles and before she can answer, he says, "Wait. Forget it. I don't want to know. Wait—one of my friends? Oh, Jesus, was it Robbie?" Grace's smile gets wider and wider until he can't look at her anymore. "I hope he's fucking dead."

"Sexting is really pedestrian anyway," Rhys declares. "What happened to love letters? E-mails. Love e-mails, sorry."

"Love letters now," I say absently. "E-mail is over."

"I just got a chill when you said that."

Lily showed me a dirty text message she got once. It said something like *I want to be inside you* but it was text-speak: *I want 2b inside u*. It made me blush and she acted like it was nothing, like it was just her life that someone would say something like that to her.

"What's it like out there?" Harrison asks.

I don't realize what he's asking and who he's asking until I look up and find everyone's gazes divided between me and Rhys. I look back down at the floor quickly because I want him to handle it. But he knows that. He knows that and he is still angry at me because he says, "I don't know. What do you think, Sloane?"

I shake my head. "I don't know either."

"Yes you do," Trace says. "Tell us what it's like out there now."

There's a beat and then—

"Quiet."

Rhys and I say it at the same time. It's such a strange thing that it would be the first word out of our mouths. I look at him and he looks at me and I feel what happened out there will connect us for as long as we're alive.

"It's quiet," Rhys says. "I can't even describe it."

They turn to me again, for confirmation, and I can only nod.

"What about when they came?" Grace asks. "I mean, I don't understand how either of you made it back. Rhys said you were outnumbered but you made it and—" She stops and I know what she's thinking. *My parents were outnumbered. They didn't make it.* "You didn't even get bitten."

"I came close," I say.

"Too close," Cary mutters.

"They're . . . they don't think like we do, you guys know that," Rhys says. "It was . . . it's not like they work together. They're dumb animals. They were fighting each other for Sloane and holding each other back. I just went at them while they were distracted. We got lucky."

"The girl was persistent," I say. As soon as I say it, I see her in my head, I see her eyes staring into mine and she's hungry, I remember that hunger, but now I remember something else: a longing like . . . no—I'm imagining that. I make myself picture her again and this time it's just hunger. That's all there is, nothing more complicated than that. It's so uncomplicated, I'd almost call it beautiful and that sounds wrong, but it's true.

"Were you scared?" Grace asks me.

I can't lie to her.

"No. I mean . . . I think when you know it's really going to happen . . . that you're really going to die, just . . . a part of you accepts it because there's nothing else you can do."

"Well, it probably helped that you were semi-conscious," Rhys says. "I bet you'd have felt differently if you were really awake."

"You think so? I don't think so."

Trace lets out an impressed whistle.

Grace says, "Well I couldn't . . . I wouldn't feel that way."

"Do you—" Harrison stops. "Do you think they have souls?"

"Oh fuck," Cary says. "Remember when we were playing I Never? That was a lot of fun and this is turning out not to be."

Nobody says anything for a long time and then Grace reaches for the bottle.

"I've never stolen from my parents."

"Really?" Trace asks.

He takes a drink. I take a drink. Cary takes a drink.

Rhys takes a drink. Even Harrison takes a drink. It's so nothing, stealing from your parents. Money went missing from my dad's wallet all the time and he never knew about it. It was the only way I could contribute because he wouldn't let me work before I turned eighteen. Lily was allowed, just not me. Arbitrary rules. Lily was at the supermarket setting aside what she could for us. But I couldn't let her do it all by herself. I touch the bandage on my head, let my finger dig into it until I feel the sting. If I'd been caught in his wallet, if he noticed the missing bills, it would've been so bad for me. Lily told me that every time I handed them to her but she still took the money because it was for our escape plan. *Our* escape plan. Our. Escape. Together.

"Okay?" Rhys asks me. I lower my hand and nod. He contemplates the bottle next and then, after a long moment says, "I have never fallen in love."

Depressing. Worse: Trace and Grace are the only ones who drink. Cary avoids my eyes and it takes me a minute to figure out why; he had sex with Lily, but didn't love her. I don't know if that kind of thing makes more or less sense to me now.

Cary grabs the bottle from Grace after she has her drink.

"Are we even deciding turns right?" I ask, confused.

Cary takes a swig out of turn. "If we're doing it wrong, we won't call it I Never. It's just sharing, Sloane. That's all it is."

"In that case." Harrison clears his throat. "I've never had sex."

I know if I don't drink, it'll just be me and Harrison, so

I take the bottle after Rhys has his go and I take a longer pull off it than I should, like I am *so totally not a virgin*.

I pass it to Grace. Trace makes retching noises as she sips.

"Sloane, you haven't gone yet," Rhys points out. "You've never I nevered."

And then the bottle is back in my hands. I don't know what to say, share. It's funny how little I've actually done of the things that are supposed to matter—kiss, sex, drugs—but I've killed a man. I've done that. I close my eyes but when I do, my brain feels a bit liquid. I sort of hate that. But it seems a fair trade-off because the whiskey has dulled my aches. I like that.

"I've never . . ." I stare at the label. "I never . . ."

"You're thinking about it too long," Trace says.

"I've never run away from home."

Cary drinks. When he was five, he explains. He didn't want to clean his room.

So we go round and round, the questions getting more perverted and inane as we do. The bottle seems endless and I feel sleepy and hot and I've lied to them all a lot because I guess I care what they think and I don't even know why I care what they think.

When Harrison passes on drink number who knows, Trace zeroes in on him.

"Man, what have you *done*?" he asks. "You take drinks when you shouldn't and you don't drink when you should. You need to do something about your . . ." Oops. It's not a sentence Trace should finish, but he does it anyway. "Life."

"How world-weary were *you* at fourteen?" Rhys asks.

"I'm not saying he should've fucked someone already," Trace says generously. He's smashed. "But I mean, Harrison, do you like—do you even know what a kiss is? Like . . . do you need someone here to explain it to you just in case it happened and you didn't know?"

"Jesus, Trace," Cary mutters. Out of all of us, he's the most gone. Or experienced, I guess. His shoulders are slumped and every so often he tilts forward like he's lost his balance, even though he's sitting. "Shut the fuck up."

"I know what a kiss is," Harrison whispers.

"He's *fourteen*," Grace says, while Harrison sits there looking devastated. "Don't be so hard on him, Trace."

"I'm fifteen," Harrison says miserably.

"Just forget it, Harrison. Please." Cary grabs the bottle. "It's not a big deal."

"But it *is*. I've never—I've never done anything. I've never had anything done to me—"

"Game over please," Cary says loudly. He takes a gulp of whiskey and swishes it around his mouth before swallowing. "Let's move on, to straight drinking."

Harrison presses his lips together, pushes his palms against the floor. He looks away from us and for once I get the impression that he is really, truly trying not to cry and it's not half-hearted or anything, his body shakes with the effort. Even Trace is quieted by it. He tries to take it all back when it's too late.

"Harrison, I was just fucking with you . . ."

"No, you weren't. It's nothing. I thought it could be something, I mean, eventually." He finally looks at us. "My life. I thought—but I mean . . . it's nothing."

Cary groans. "Please shut up."

"But I still want it to be something," Harrison says. A single tear trails down his cheek. "That's stupid, isn't it? And now it's too late to do anything about it."

Cary buries his head in his hands. No one does or says anything for a long time and then Grace scoots over to Harrison. Her nose and cheeks are a warm red from the whiskey. She wraps an arm around him and he starts to cry in earnest.

"Don't cry," she says. "You have a lot of time."

"No, I don't."

"Yeah, you do."

"No—"

"Yeah! Yeah, you do. It's okay. Look—"

She does something that is amazingly selfless and also gross. She tilts Harrison's face up and gives him a sweet kiss on the lips and it lasts long enough for him to taste her back, to move his mouth against hers. Trace regards her proudly and when it's over, Harrison stares at her dumbfounded but he's stopped crying.

She is so nice.

Cary makes a disgusted noise and struggles to his feet. "Well, this was fun until Harrison started crying, but hey. That's what he does, right? Thanks, Harrison."

This brings Harrison back. "I didn't—"

"Yeah, you did."

"What the fuck is your problem?" Trace asks. "Let the kid cry if he needs to."

"That's all we let Harrison do! I don't want to *dwell*."

Cary rubs his eyes. "I'm tired of dwelling. I just wanted to get totally wasted and—"

"You're there," Rhys tells him.

"It was just sharing," I say. "That's all he did."

"Yeah, but not—" Cary gestures to Harrison. It throws him off balance. He sways precariously for a second before steadying himself. "Not *that*. We didn't need to hear it. I didn't want to hear it. It's fucking pathetic . . ."

"I'm sorry," Harrison says. "I didn't mean to—"

"He can fucking dwell if he wants to," Trace says. "I never see *you* dwell."

"Oh, let me guess," Cary replies. "The next words out of your mouth are going to be something about your dead parents that I killed because I'm a murderer."

"Yeah, something like that. Exactly like that actually."

They stare at each other. I watch Trace. He holds Cary's gaze, unblinking. Cary caves first and he does it in a way I don't expect, that I don't think any of us expect. He curls his hand into a fist and presses it against his forehead.

"You think I wanted this," he says.

"Cary," Grace starts. "Don't do this—"

"But you must. You think I wanted it," he says. "You actually think I wanted to be left *with* you guys, *without* them." He laughs. "You think I wanted that? *Really?*" He takes a step back. "I didn't. I loved the idea of—I loved the idea of them." He lowers his hand. "It shouldn't have been them. It should have been—"

He stares at us, lost, and I keep waiting for him to finish

even though I know he's never going to finish. *It should've been me.* Cary changes for me in that instant. From the boy who is crazy good at survival stuff to the boy who thinks he should be dead.

He's finally become someone I understand.

He shakes his head and weaves out of the auditorium. He's through with us, with everything. I want to follow after him, tell him he's not alone.

I want to ask him how we can help each other.

Grace catches my eye. She opens her mouth and closes it and then she looks away. She doesn't look happy anymore. I feel like someone should do something. I guess it should be me. I get to my feet and the world tilts a little.

"I'll find him."

"Don't," Trace says. "Let him rot."

Rhys stands. "I'll go with you."

I don't want his company but I guess I'm stuck with it. Rhys is steadier on his feet than I am and when we leave the auditorium, I end up following him. He seems to know where Cary is: the library. He's slumped over at one of the tables, his head resting in his arms.

"Just leave me alone," he slurs. "Please."

"Let us take you back to your mat," Rhys says.

"Mat. I don't even have a *bed* anymore. None of us have beds anymore. You realize this, right? We can't go home. There are no more beds." He raises his head and looks at us. His eyes are glassy. "We can't go home, Sloane."

"That's okay with me."

"Why? *This* is the alternative."

"Okay. Enough." Rhys stands behind Cary and pulls

him to his feet. Cary pushes away from him and says, "I am *not* going back to the auditorium—"

"The nurse's office, then," Rhys says.

So we take him there. Cary needs an arm around each of us to stay upright. Taking on his weight slows us down. His legs are uncooperative, jelly, and as we pass a classroom, he detours inside and pukes in a garbage can and then he spits.

"Better," he mumbles. After that, he is a little better. He just wants to pass out, he tells us. When we hit the nurse's office, he flops back on the cot and Rhys unties his shoes.

"I'm a murderer," Cary says. "I. Am. A. Murderer."

"No, you're drunk. Sleep it off."

I don't want Cary to stop talking. I want him to finish what he was going to say in the auditorium. I want to hear someone else say they've given up. I need to hear it.

"It should've been you, right?"

Rhys gives me a look. "Sloane."

"What? No . . ." Cary blinks. "No. It should've been—Harrison."

"That kid just can't get a break," Rhys says.

"We didn't even *know* him—" Cary sits up with difficulty. "Rhys, remember we found him and we didn't know him and it turns out he went to this fucking school? Just by looking at him, you could tell he's nothing. Everyone else—everyone else, we knew—" He leans forward and puts his head between his knees. "It should have been Harrison."

"You'd feel just as bad as you do now if it had been."

"No one would have held it against me if it had been Harrison."

Cary's breathing gets so heavy and for a second I think he's passed out sitting up, but then his shoulders start to shake. He's crying.

I turn to Rhys, who stares at Cary, horrified. Rhys turns to me and his eyes are begging me to do something, like I'm the girl here and I should know what to do. I take a tentative step toward Cary but I don't know what to do. I think I'd need to be drunker than I am to have any idea of what to do or say to help him. Cary raises his head and he looks so sad.

"The alley *was* swarmed," he whispers. My heart hears this, processes it, understands it before my brain does. I take two steps back. "I knew it was swarmed . . ."

"Cary, shut up," Rhys says.

"It was the only way to the school and none of us knew Harrison. Bait."

"Cary."

"But the Caspers insisted, you know? They insisted, didn't they? They couldn't wait and I—I couldn't say I lied, right? But it wasn't . . . it wasn't supposed to be them. It was supposed to be Harrison. I set it up and it was supposed to be . . . Harrison—"

He starts to sob. He cries so hard I think he'll be sick again. He curls up on his side, his eyes squeezed shut. The pain is so etched on his face that I can feel it. He knew that the alley was swarmed.

Harrison was bait.

And I remember—I remember Cary looking down that alley and turning back to us, telling us it was safe and the

Caspers . . . the Caspers rushing ahead. They wanted to get to the school so badly, they were so eager for the walls, the shelter to keep them and their children safe. I close my eyes and I hear Mrs. Casper's voice in my head, just before she went. *Thank God one thing's finally gone right.* She sounded so hopeful, so relieved. And then—

"Cary," Rhys says.

"Go. Just get the fuck away from me—"

Rhys doesn't need more incentive than that. He grabs me by the hand and pulls me out of the nurse's office. He shuts the door quietly and then stares through the window at Cary. My heart is jackhammering in my chest. Rhys turns to me.

"We can't tell anyone about this."

"I know."

"I'm serious, Sloane. We can't—"

"I *know.*"

He swallows, nods, and then we make our way down the hall together, back to the auditorium. I am terrified they'll somehow see what I've heard on my face, so I stop. Rhys stops. He waits for me to walk again and I do and he walks with me. When we turn the corner, I realize how spent I am. I lean against a locker. I really don't want to go back. Not yet.

"Are you okay?" he asks.

"Give me a minute."

"Whiskey and head trauma don't really go, huh."

"I don't want to be around you right now."

The meanness surprises the boy who told me to kill

myself, but wouldn't let me kill myself. He stalks off. I wait until he's gone and then I sit down on the floor.

My father never went after Lily after she left. Nineteen. She was legally an adult, but he was so angry I could never understand why he didn't just go to the police and make them track her down. I don't know why he didn't make it hard for her. But then I think . . . as long as he had something to hurt it must've been okay that she was gone. Cary wanted to use Harrison as bait and the Caspers got in the way. The Caspers thought Cary should stand in front of them. They thought he was expendable. The man outside, he was expendable. He didn't mean anything to me. Was I expendable? Was I Lily's bait?

I go to the bathroom and splash water on my face. My head feels awful. When I finally get to the auditorium, I stretch out on my mat. Grace is on Trace's mat and Trace and Harrison are across the room, eating a bag of chips. Harrison is talking and Trace is actually listening to him. Trace must feel bad about bringing the wrath of Cary down on Harrison or else he's really drunk because I can't think of any other reason why he'd care what Harrison has to say.

Harrison was supposed to die.

"How bad is he?"

Grace's voice pulls me from my thoughts.

"Who?"

"Cary," she says.

"Why do you care?"

"Just tell me how he is."

I want to tell her he's bad. I want to tell her Cary's not

the guy she thinks he is, that he's simultaneously better and worse than anything she's imagined, but I can't.

"He was crying his eyes out."

"Yeah right."

"I've never seen a boy cry like that before. Not even Harrison."

She considers this. "But he's wasted, so it doesn't mean anything."

"Maybe it's the only way it could come out."

"Sure."

I can't deal with this. Her. The pounding in my head. Trace. Cary. Her. Harrison is supposed to be dead. *I'm* supposed to be dead.

"You and Trace make a game out of hating Cary. He feels it."

"You think I should forgive him? You think that's important now?"

"I think you still have something and he doesn't have anything and he told you both he was sorry." I close my eyes. There is no buzz anymore, if there ever was, just tiredness curdling my blood. "And I think he is."

"He only said it once."

"Is it going to make a difference if he says it a million times?"

"I never saw him cry."

"Then go into the nurse's office."

"You're not being fair."

"He said—" I stop, and then I lie. Maybe it will help. "He said it should've been him."

"He didn't."

"Fine, Grace." I roll onto my side, putting my back to her. "He didn't."

Eventually, the sun goes down. We call it a night long before that.

I'm standing on the edge of a cliff and it feels like my heart is missing.

Sloane.

Post-whiskey, my head is thick and my eyes are weighted. I can barely open them, but still I hear his voice, calling for me. I should let him know I hear him calling for me.

"Dad—"

The moment the word is out of my mouth, I'm awake

and I want to be sick. There's a difference in saying it out loud on purpose and having it involuntarily twitch its way past my lips. *Dad.* I sit up slowly and check my watch. Five in the morning. Rhys shifts and rolls over. His face is smooth, untouched. Everyone around me is still, hours away from their eyes being open and I'm jealous because I just want to be asleep like them. In this moment, that is the only thing I want.

Footsteps.

Outside the auditorium.

At first, I think *Cary.* Cary, wandering his way back from the nurse's office. Those footsteps are his. But they're not. They are heavy and uneven, familiar in a way that makes my skin crawl. A hand against my face. *Dad?* They get closer. A shadow moves across the floor as it passes by the door. I jerk my head in the direction of the hall, see the last of the shadow drift away. A person. That was real. No. I press my hand against my chest, feel myself working. My breathing is shallow, a sick juxtaposition against Rhys's soft and steady breaths in and out. I just saw someone. I know I did.

No. Something is wrong with me. I went outside and I came back broken and now my heart is trying to convince me I just saw my father walking the halls. I'm losing my mind. This feeling circles me until I get to my feet and my legs feel so strange I start to wonder if I'm actually awake after all. When I pinch my arm, I feel pain but—I tiptoe over to Grace and shake her shoulder lightly until her eyes open.

"Sloane?" She blinks. "What's wrong?"

"Am I awake?"

"What?"

"I mean—did you hear something?"

She rubs her eyes. "No—I was *asleep*. What's going on?"

"Nothing. Nothing. I'm sorry. Go back to sleep—"

"Sloane—"

"Forget it."

"No, what was—"

"It's *nothing*," I say. "I'm sorry. I think I was having a nightmare."

She glares at me through half-lidded eyes and rolls over. I stand in the center of the room, not knowing what to do next. I can't go back to sleep. I was dead asleep and then I wasn't and I heard—no, I didn't hear anything. I did not hear anything.

I sit on my mat and try to calm down. I last a minute before I'm back on my feet. I grab a flashlight and walk to the bathroom and stand at the sinks with my hands on the hot and cold taps. My heart does a little dance before twisting them on. How much water is left in the tank? How much did they use up in the shower, trying to get all the infected blood off me? How much was in it when we got here? I cup my hands under the stream and splash my face. The last of sleep is washed away and I'm really awake now and I'm not sure that was a smart thing to do. I keep the tap running for a minute and lean against the stall and listen to it, even though I shouldn't. For some reason, the sound of the wasted water makes me think of birds singing in trees. I wonder if there are birds anymore. I brush that stupid thought away.

Of course there are.

I turn the water off and leave the bathroom. Instead of heading back to the auditorium, I wander in the opposite direction, where I thought I heard the footsteps I imagined go.

I don't know why I need to chase this nightmare.

The sound of my bare feet against the cold floors is unnerving. It makes me walk faster. I end up at the back of the school, facing the barricaded doors outside, the ones that lead to the athletic field. I get as close to the doors as I possibly can, squeezing myself past desks which nearly make up the width of the hall. I wedge myself into a space and rest my head against the wall. I don't know what I'm doing. I stay there so long, my legs lock and my neck and shoulders start to ache. I can't hear anything outside.

It's been so quiet since the gas station.

I wonder what it looks like out there. I wonder what my house looks like. I miss my room, my bed. In my room, at home, I slept with the window open in the summer, listened to the cars go by, to the leaves on the maple outside rustling against each other when the wind was just right. Lily used to sneak out through my window, scale that tree up and down . . .

Someone is behind me.

I whirl around. My side connects with the edge of a desk. I double over, briefly forgetting everything but the pain until I raise my head and I see a man. A bulky frame, familiar. His back is to me. This *is* real. No. How can I tell if this is real when I don't even know what real is anymore? There is a man at the end of this hall. No, I'm asleep. I

close my eyes. Open them. Still there. Close my eyes. Open. Still there.

"Dad?" I call. "Dad—"

The man squares his shoulders. He begins a slow turn, but I feel like if I see him the world is going to come down on me. I don't want to see him. I can't. I turn the flashlight off and run blindly back to the auditorium and then I'm at Grace's side, shaking her awake again.

"Grace, wake up, wake up, please, please, *please*—there's something—there's someone in the school, someone got in—"

I sit on my mat with Grace's arm around me, while Cary, Rhys, and Trace shuffle in after doing a sweep of the building. Cary is rumpled but awake, very hung over, and judging by the way he's looking at me, so not impressed. I don't care. I pick at my fingernails, trying to distract myself because if I don't, I will lose it. Harrison is on Grace's other side. He's too terrified to talk, was too terrified to help the others look. But there's nothing for him or me to worry about because there is no one else in this school. No one else is in this school.

No one.

"It's just us." Cary rubs his eyes. "Jesus, I could have used twelve more hours."

I bury my head in my knees.

"It's okay," Grace says, rubbing my back. I melt at her warmth. It goes straight to the deadest parts of me. "It was probably a nightmare."

"How's your head feel?" Rhys asks.

"Go to hell," I mutter. I feel Grace's surprise and then I forget the only two people that know Rhys and I are not okay right now are me and Rhys.

"I'm just saying—"

"It's not *that*."

But maybe it is that.

"Has it happened before?" Grace asks.

This is the worst moment, walking myself into that question. My silence is as good as *yes* and then she starts in with this gentle line of questioning—*when, where were you, how did you feel*. I go as far back as the nurse's office in my recounting but I don't tell them about those first few days after we got here when I imagined his cologne. Except if I knew the cologne wasn't real and I think this is, then maybe I *did* hear someone in the hall, I did.

Didn't I?

"No one could get in," Cary says firmly. "We made sure of that."

It's morning. When I look at the windows overhead, the

sky is gray-white and I think it might rain. Maybe they're right. No one is in this school. Maybe it's just me, my head.

"I'm sorry," I say.

Cary crouches in front of me. His closeness sends Grace to her feet. She moves away from both of us. There is this moment before she goes, though, where her eyes meet his.

"You've been hurt. You got scared," Cary says. "It happens."

It happened.

Everyone treats me way too nicely because of the things I think I've seen. They don't want me to feel awkward but it makes me feel awkward. I last about half the morning in their company, trying to act more okay than I feel when the whole charade starts to get to me and I excuse myself. I decide to retrace my steps last night and I'm all of five minutes alone before Rhys shows. I want to tell him to go away, but what does it matter. He'll always be here.

All of us will always be here.

This place is a coffin.

"So are you trying to scare us all out of the school?" Rhys asks. "Am I going to have to watch you to make sure you're not going to fuck with us so you can find some dramatic way to leave?" I don't say anything and he studies me. "If you're not lying, it could be a concussion or something. Underneath that bandage, you're missing a chunk of your forehead. It's probably going to scar."

My hand moves to the bandage. I push at it.

The sting is so sour I can almost taste it.

"Why are you out here?" I ask him.

"Why are you?" he asks back.

I've reached the end of the hall and I'm at the classroom door I saw the man standing at. I push it open. It's Mr. Baxter's room. My annoyance at Rhys disappears when I step inside. I move down an aisle of desks, touching my hands to them as I pass. The wrongness of it all creeps up on me. I don't want to forget the function of this place.

I don't want to forget how it used to be.

I reach Baxter's desk and sit in his chair while Rhys stands in the center of the room, watching. There's an agenda in front of me. Who uses things like these anymore when there are smartphones? I flip to a random page and see an appointment for the dentist, but right underneath that it says *Madeline this morning: red nightgown* and I am overcome by how personal these five words are. It reminds me of Lily telling me how our mom used to use the calendar on the bulletin board in the kitchen like a diary. Appointments noted, yes, but also little tidbits like *girls fought—Sloane took Lily's dolls!* Lily said Mom saved them all and I asked Dad about them once, but he wouldn't tell me where he kept them, or even if he did . . .

"Guilt," Rhys says.

I look up. "What?"

"The man you saw. I bet it's because you feel guilty about the guy outside."

"Oh, really."

"I'm not being an asshole," he says. "I'm just saying

maybe that's why you thought you saw someone. Like it's . . . stress. Guilt."

"But I don't feel guilty about the man." It's a lie but I balance it with truth. "I'm jealous."

"He's *turned*, Sloane. He's out there right now."

"I know."

Rhys is losing weight, I notice that now. His cheekbones are so sharp, sharper than I remember them being before and he already has an angular face. We're wasting away.

"You really think there's nothing left for us?" he asks.

"I think there's nothing left for me. I don't think that for everyone else."

"So what do they have that you don't at this point?"

I press my lips together. I don't want to talk about this anymore. I don't want to talk about how everyone has something even if they don't really have it anymore, that what they *had* makes them strong enough for this, to keep going.

"Guilt," Rhys repeats.

"I didn't see *that* man. It was—"

Shut up. *Shut up.*

"Who did you think it was?" His voice is quiet now like we're in a church. There's a determined look in his eyes. I know he'll push this until he gets an answer, so I just tell him.

"My father. I thought—him."

"I thought your father was dead."

"I hope he is." I swallow. "I wish it."

I make him speechless. It's a nicer feeling than it should be. He doesn't get it. He doesn't get how I could sit here and say something like that and mean it. But why would he. His home life was probably—not like mine. I bet it was perfect. I bet even the worst parts of it were better than mine. Before he can ask more, Cary steps into the room, breathless.

"I've been looking all over for you," he says. "I just want to get this out of the way now. What I said yesterday—"

"No one's going to say anything," I tell him.

He relaxes. "Okay. Good."

I flip Baxter's agenda open and closed while they just stand there. Flip to the first page. Nick Baxter. Phone and cell phone numbers. Address. Nick Baxter.

Nick.

"Oh," I say.

"What?" Rhys asks.

The world breaks into a million pieces and comes back together just as quickly but it comes back together wrong. The picture is wrong. Upside down, awful. I stand slowly and move around Baxter's desk, instinct guiding me. I feel like my brain is shutting down or waking up in a way it's never been awake before. I move along the back of the room and come to the closet. I open the door and everything stops. Everything. Rhys and Cary get so quiet, I'm afraid they disappeared or they were never here at all and I think I made this moment happen, I willed this man into existence.

Mr. Baxter.

He's curled up on the floor, asleep. He's not even a ghost of the person he used to be. There is nothing of our teacher left in him. That steady, solid frame that stood over all of us and kept us quiet has now shrunk in on itself, somehow. His cheeks are hollow and his face is so pale that if he wasn't breathing, I'd think he was dead. He's wearing a suit. A dress shirt, ripped and covered in blood and muck. He's *alive*. Seeing someone else in this school, alive, is almost too much. I'm afraid of it. I'm afraid of this ravaged man.

"Get the gun, Sloane," Rhys says.

I'm too shocked to understand what he's saying.

"The gun—*get it!*"

That's when I notice the handgun resting in Baxter's lap. It's angled weirdly toward me, sends my heart into a furious rhythm. I reach forward slowly. My fingers get way too close to my English teacher's crotch in the process and that alone makes my stomach turn. Mr. Baxter's eyes flicker. I scramble back with the gun in my hands and Rhys is behind me, ripping it from my grasp, which makes me realize all the things I can do with a gun.

"Holy shit," Rhys says.

I'm so overcome with the urge to say *I told you so. I told you someone was in here.* Then my brain spazzes out. *Someone else is in here. Someone else got in.*

Rhys and Cary stare at this lump of a human being— another human being in this school with us, an *adult*— and have no idea what to do.

Cary turns to us. "How did he get in?" Before either of

us can answer, he strides forward and kicks Baxter, who is slowly waking up, in the legs.

"*Cary—*" Rhys reaches for him, but it's too late.

Baxter moans. Cary nudges him with his foot again and I move farther away because I don't want to be close to this. I want to be as far from it as I can.

"Sloane, get back here," Rhys says.

The gun. Rhys has the gun. *We* have a gun. No, Baxter has a gun. It's Baxter's gun. This is Baxter's classroom. Is this Baxter's school? Does he have more right to it than we do because he works here? Worked here? I can't get my brain to stop from wondering frantically because it doesn't know what matters anymore, what is the most important thing. The most important thing: Baxter is alive. He's in this school and he's alive.

"Baxter," Cary says, and then he corrects himself. "Mr. Baxter—"

Baxter is awake now, staring at us with empty eyes. Fleeting recognition passes through them. He opens his mouth to speak but Cary cuts him off.

"How did you get in here? You have to tell us how you got in—"

"You found me," Baxter says. Just listening to the words scrape through his mouth makes me thirsty. "I wondered when you'd find me . . ."

"Mr. Baxter, how did you get in here?"

"My gun—where is my gun? Which one of you took it?"

Rhys hides the gun behind his back. Cary crouches down directly in front of Baxter and takes his face in his hands. "Listen to me: How. Did. You. Get. In. Here?"

Baxter stares at Cary for a long time.

"I don't know," he says, and then his body goes slack. Cary steps back, letting the man slump into nothing. The dull sound of his breathing fills the room.

Baxter is weak.

While we've been making ourselves comfortable in here, he's been running and starving, seeking shelter in the least obvious places he can find. *Surviving,* he says, and the word is bitter out of his mouth. We give him food. He eats canned peaches and throws them up. He drinks a bottle of water and throws it up too. We find antacids in the nurse's office and he's able to keep a bit of food and water down after that. He tells us he was on his "last leg" before he got here. His eyes are dull, cloudy and he can't hold on to a thought long enough to say anything useful. Every time he speaks, there's something so sad about the way his voice sounds. I can't believe there was a time he stood in front of a classroom and taught us.

This man is Mr. Baxter but he's not Mr. Baxter anymore.

"The barricades are incredible." He looks at us, something akin to pride in his eyes. "An incredible testament . . . to teenage ingenuity. Look at how safe we are."

"We're *not* safe," Cary says. This will be the thousandth time he tries to direct Baxter's attention to the most important situation at hand. "If you got in, those things outside can too."

"I know, Mr. Chen. I know that—"

"Then you know it's life and death. We *need* to know how you got in."

Baxter closes his eyes and then opens them. "I can't remember . . ."

"But you remember being in this school," Rhys says. "You don't remember getting in, but you remember being in here after you got in."

"Just pieces. Price," Baxter says. "I remember seeing Ms. Price . . ." They all look at me when he says this and I feel sick when I remember his hand on my face as I slept. I want to ask him why he did that, but I don't think I really want to know. "But it all feels like—the same day." He licks his lips. They're so raw, cracked. "Every day feels the same."

"You could've shown yourself," Rhys tells him. "You had a gun."

"You outnumber me and I didn't know what you'd been through. How long you were here . . . what you were capable of . . ."

"We're not infected," Harrison says. "We wouldn't have hurt you."

Mr. Baxter looks at Harrison in total wonderment and then he laughs. It's a bad sound, wrong. It makes me shiver.

"Does the water still work?" he asks. "The tank still has water in it?"

Trace nods. "Do you know how full it was before this started?"

Baxter shakes his head.

"Mr. Baxter?" Grace steps forward, nervous. "What's it like out there? Is it—is it much worse than it was? Or is it getting better at all?"

"Sometimes . . . it seems safer than it is," he says. "They wait, now. If they can't find life, they seem to wait for it. That's why it's quieter. It's quiet but it's not safer."

I glance at Rhys.

Quiet.

"What do they eat?" I ask. "When there are no people?"

"I've seen them eat animals. Anything . . . living."

"You seriously can't remember how you got in?" Cary asks.

"*Cary,*" Grace snaps. "Just give him a minute—"

"Grace, a minute could be the difference between us being *ripped apart*—"

"The gun," Baxter interrupts. "If something happens, it should help. Where is it?"

"You know what? Mr. Baxter needs a minute, you're right," Cary says abruptly. "We can talk about this after. Rhys, Sloane, I want to search the first floor for his way in. I don't imagine he scaled the wall and got in through the roof, right, Mr. B?"

"I don't imagine," Baxter echoes.

"So we'll find it and we'll seal it." Cary turns to the others. Trace and Grace stare at him contemptuously. Cary's directive to them has to be something they can't argue with. Something simple. "Make sure Mr. Baxter has everything he needs. Mr. Baxter, I want you to work as hard as you can to remember in the meantime."

"Amazing," Baxter says at our backs as Cary, Rhys, and I make our way out of the room. "If only you'd shown that kind of initiative in my class, Mr. Chen."

"You're sounding better by the second, sir," Cary replies without turning.

When we hit the hall, Cary mouths *library*. Rhys and I head one way and Cary heads the other. I don't know why we can't go there together. Cary gets there before us. He's checking the room for Baxter's way in. We wait until he's finished.

"It's not here," he says, frustrated. "Rhys, you hid the gun?"

"Yeah. It's—" Rhys stops himself. "It's someplace safe. I'll show you later."

Cary glances at Rhys and then me but he doesn't pursue it.

"I don't trust him," he says.

"Cary, you don't *like* him," I say. "You never did. He never liked you."

"Yeah, and that has nothing to do with *this*. This is fucked. We have to timeline it. He hasn't been here since we got here, right?"

"I don't think so," I say. "I think he got in before Rhys and I went out . . . I mean, not by days or anything. I'm talking minutes, maybe a half an hour to an hour, I don't know."

"Why do you think that?"

"The man outside." I glance at Rhys. "He called for *Nick* over and over . . . and Mr. Baxter's first name is Nick."

We're quiet for a moment, and then Rhys speaks. "So if he got here with that guy, he left him out there to die. Something bad must have happened between them."

"But that man was unconscious when we found him," I say. "We thought he was dead. Maybe Mr. Baxter did too and went on without him . . ."

"Or maybe Baxter hurt him," Cary suggests.

I shake my head. "He wouldn't do that."

"Why not? He hasn't said anything about the guy outside yet. If it was innocent, why wouldn't he just get it out of the way and say so?"

"He's hardly said *anything*. He's out of it. Shell-shocked."

"*Is* he, though?" Rhys asks.

"Wait." I can't keep up with this. "You think he's faking it?"

"You really think he can't remember how he got in this school?" Rhys looks at me like he can't believe I haven't come to all the conclusions they have in the hour Baxter has been here. "How do you forget something like that?"

I cross my arms. "*Why* would he do that?"

"Who knows why anyone does anything now?" Cary looks past me and Rhys, to the door, and we both turn. There's no one there but Cary lowers his voice anyway. "If he's had some bad experiences with other survivors, he could be looking at his way in as leverage. He needs to make sure we trust him."

"Right . . . we keep him around no matter what, hoping that it will eventually come to him because we can't find it ourselves," Rhys says. "When he's sure he's safe here, he tells us or . . . he holds it over our heads for the entire time we're here."

"He thinks he can just come in and take over," Cary mutters.

"We've been in this room, what, ten minutes and we're already saddling the guy with a bunch of sinister motivations," I say. "This is our *English teacher*. Someone we *know*."

"*We* all know each other and we don't trust each other," Cary says. "The only people I trust in this building are you and Rhys. The rest are dead weight to me."

"But maybe . . ." I grope desperately for some kind of explanation for Baxter's behavior that seems more human. "Maybe Baxter was going to come to the school with the guy outside but they got separated or he really did think the guy was dead. Maybe he's so traumatized he can't remember how he got in. Why isn't that possible?"

They both stare at me and I can tell I've disappointed them. I don't know why I don't just believe what they believe. I don't know why I'm defending Baxter. I think of his hand on my face. Maybe I should tell them but I can't. It makes me feel too weird. It would just make things worse.

"Whatever," Cary finally says. "None of that matters yet. The only thing that matters right now is how he got in."

We can't find it.

We look everywhere, scour classrooms, the custodian's office. We go into the basement and it's so dark in there, the weak light from our flashlights turn the sinks and the shelves against the far wall into terrifying shadows. I wonder if Baxter is some sort of group hallucination but I know he's not. I also know the other barricades are holding, undisturbed, and there is absolutely no way he got past them. How did he get in? I check the closet we found him in halfheartedly, like it might hold a secret passageway but it doesn't. Of course it doesn't.

The building is officially one less place we can trust.

Cary heads back to the auditorium wringing his hands, trying to figure out a good way to break bad news. Rhys wanders off and I can tell he's taking this hard. We survived outside once and then again despite my better efforts, and then we got back inside and we thought we were safe but we're not safe. Everything is up in the air. He doesn't want to die.

I seek him out and find him in the gym, opening a pack of cigarettes. He places one between his lips and brings a lighter to it. The flame flickers, illuminating his face briefly, before the smoke drifts lazily around him. He shoves the half-crumpled pack in his pocket. He doesn't say anything to me, but he knows I'm here. I don't say anything to him, just watch him inhale like a pro. I close the distance between us. When he exhales, he takes care to turn his head from me and I'm struck by how attractive and easy he makes it look but he always made it look that way.

"I just had this vision of you out front, smoking," I say.

"That was my thing." He ashes the cigarette. "What do you want, Sloane?"

I stare out at the bleachers. It used to give me hives, imagining myself on any kind of team, people looking at me. "If Baxter got in here two days ago, that means however he got in here has been open since we got here. None of the infected found their way in."

"Are you trying to make me feel better?"

"Where did you hide the gun?"

"I'm not telling you."

"Promise I'm not going to shoot myself in the face."

"Why should I take you at your word? You threw yourself into a bunch of infected. Blowing a bullet through your skull seems way less hardcore so why wouldn't you go for it? It's that much easier for you."

"What do you think you'd do with my body?" I ask, and he twitches, steps away from me. I've crossed some invisible line. "Oh, what? It's okay for you to be so candid with me?" I stare at the ceiling and think about it. "You couldn't just leave it here to decompose. That would probably be unsafe. Taking it outside would be even more dangerous . . ."

"It must thrill you that there's a secret way in here," Rhys shoots back. "That one day we could wake up and be totally surrounded—"

"The way you look at things is *so* uncomplicated."

"Oh, I'm so sorry I've pegged you all wrong." He raises a hand. "I take it back. You're not thrilled we could wake up one day and be totally surrounded."

"I'm not thrilled. I'm not anything."

Rhys drops the cigarette on the floor and grinds it out.

"Wasn't your dad though, was it."

"No."

"You know, if I thought it was mine, like even for a second—even if I knew, rationally, it couldn't be him—" He stops and shrugs. "Fuck it. Never mind."

He takes out the pack of cigarettes again, but this time he holds it out. I shake my head. He shrugs but he doesn't look away, just keeps his eyes on me until I'm so uncomfortable I feel I have to be the first of us to leave to win this moment between us, so I do.

Baxter sits in the chair at the head of the table and starts nodding off and then Trace and Rhys help him to his own mat so he can sleep for a bit. We move quietly around him. We don't even talk. He's already leveled our dynamic and Harrison is the only one who seems happy about it. He should be devastated about this new unknown way into the school but instead, he's *happy*. It's easy to understand why because Harrison is really simple. This is what Harrison thinks: Baxter will remember soon and then he'll recover and he'll take care of us.

I watch Baxter sleep. He moans and jerks awake.

"The radio," he says groggily.

"You've heard it?" Trace asks.

"Once. Has it changed? I doubt it has . . ."

Trace crosses the room and switches the radio on. It's static for a few minutes and then that woman's voice comes through, loud and clear.

"*—Not a test—*"

Baxter holds up a hand and closes his eyes. Trace turns the radio off.

Around dinner, we rouse Baxter again. He sits at the head of the table—Cary's spot—and watches as Harrison and Grace bring in two trays of food.

"So you banded together. Got here all by yourselves,"

Baxter says as we settle around him. I hate the way it feels. This is *our* place but he's at the head of *our* table. In the best chair—the one we snagged from LaVallee's office. "You survived."

"Not all of us," Trace says. "Our parents. We lost them."

"I'm so sorry to hear that. How?"

"Excuse me?"

"How did they die?"

Cary is reaching for a bag of chips when Mr. Baxter asks this. His hand freezes over it, totally suspended for the briefest second, and then he grabs it and rips it open. This does not escape Baxter's notice.

"It was—" Trace starts, and I can tell he's ready to lay into Cary something fierce, which is the worst thing he could do. I brace myself but he never finishes and when I look, Grace's hand is on his arm. She's silenced him.

"We were overwhelmed," she says. "That's all."

"Yes. That happens." Baxter reaches for some rice cakes and gazes at them, like he can't believe they're real. "Did you try to get to the community center?"

"Yeah," Harrison says. "We almost didn't make it."

"We thought it would be safe," Trace says. "I guess everyone did. It was the first place we headed, right? First one gone. If we had known, we wouldn't have even tried."

"We made the same mistake," Baxter says.

"We?" I ask.

He closes his eyes and then he opens them.

"You know, we could stay here for so long if we wanted to. Even if the water tank goes, there's bottled. We could stay here as long as it takes for help to come. That's what we could do. What we *should* do. Until . . . help comes."

"Or the infected figure out the way you got in," Cary says.

"They won't."

"Then you remember where?"

Baxter shakes his head and then he says, "I just know that where we are and what we have is better than what's out there. We should hold on to it as long as possible."

Everyone murmurs in agreement, but I can't. My appetite is gone. I can't shake the feeling something is very wrong.

I get to my feet. "I'm just going to go to the bathroom . . ."

"You know what?" Grace stands. "Me too."

In the bathroom, she hovers while I splash water on my face and my neck. I try to get her to go back to the auditorium but she won't. She asks if I'm okay.

"I'm fine. Headache. Short-circuiting. I don't know."

She doesn't say anything, which is awkward. It looks like she wants to. I press my head against the mirrors. Cold. I like that.

"Can I get you anything?"

"No. I just don't want to go back out there yet. Baxter's freaking me out."

"When Cary and Rhys walked him in, Trace thought it was our dad."

"Did you?"

"No. I don't like this, though, Sloane." At first, I think she's talking about Baxter being here, but she's not. "What if they get in the school? I mean, what if—what if it's my dad or my mom the next time? What if they come in?"

"Grace, the odds of that happening—"

"Must be as good as the odds of *Baxter* getting in here after all this time, right?" There's nothing I can say to that. Tears fill her eyes. "God, when will this stop feeling so bad?"

"I don't think it does." I stare at my reflection. "I think it's just going to be like this."

She rips a swath of paper towels from the dispenser and wipes at her eyes.

"I just want to be less of a mess. I sneak in here, like, ten times a day to cry." She laughs weakly. "I wish I was like you. Strong."

I look away from my reflection. "What?"

"You just handle this. Every time I look at you, you're just taking it. And then you went outside like it was nothing. And everyone tiptoes around me. No one else made me think about laying off Cary the way you did . . . no one else made me feel *bad* for him. It's like you see things how they need to be and you're not afraid to call it."

"You're giving me way too much credit."

"I want to be more like that."

"You have more," I say. Her forehead crinkles. I can't believe she thinks I'm strong, that this is strength. "I always wanted to be like you. I still do."

"I thought you hated me," she says.

"What?"

"Sophomore year." She tosses the crumpled paper towels into the garbage. "You slept over. I thought it was great and then you stopped talking to me. I called and your sister said you didn't want to speak to me anymore. I could never figure out what I did."

The room does a slow rotation. I want to reach out for something, steady myself, but I'm frozen.

"I didn't know she did that."

"How could you not?"

"I didn't. I swear I didn't know Lily did that, Grace."

Grace studies me. "Where is she now, anyway?"

"She ran away. Six months ago," I say. When Grace's expression morphs into something pitying, I shrug and look away. "I'm sure she's fine."

"I'm so sorry, Sloane. I can't even imagine being here without Trace," she says. "And you two were as close we were . . ."

"Right. Were." I pull at a strand of my hair. I want to rip it out. I want to climb onto the roof and throw myself off it. I want to bash my head against the mirror until it breaks. "That's past tense."

She seems awed, like I'm more than what I am, like I'm not imagining a thousand different ways I could end it all right now and trying to remember why I can't.

"See? You just accept."

And then it's just me and my former English teacher.

The dinner trays are cleared from the table, the garbage is thrown away. The others decide to search for how Baxter got in. Cary's going to give them the rundown on everything we've managed to piece together about what happened before Baxter got in and the possibility that he's lying and then we'll all be suspicious. I stayed behind because I feel sick and tired and Cary said it's good if one of us stays because it will prevent Baxter from getting suspicious of our suspicion of him. Rhys said it might make him more suspicious and then *suspicious* stopped seeming like a real word. I can't tell if Cary is enjoying this or not, but I feel like he might be. I know he's worried about how Baxter got in but it's like the rest of it, the paranoia, is just something to do so he can feel like he's doing something.

"Do you think you could get me some water?" Baxter is still sitting at the table and I'm on my mat and I don't know why he can't do that for himself but I get him a bottle of water and bring it to him. He sets it on the table and then he grabs me and his fingers are as rough against my wrist as they were against my face. I swallow.

"You're hurt," he says. "The others aren't. Did they do this to you?"

"They?" My stomach turns when I realize what he's suggesting. "No."

He holds my gaze and then he lets my wrist go. I exhale and resist the urge to rub it. I walk back to my mat and sit down on it instead.

"It's good, then, that you've found people you can trust."

"I guess," I say.

"That's a rare thing at a time like this."

"Is it?"

"I think so," he says, and then he starts to ramble. "Panic reduces people to ruin. Cortege is gone and so are most of its residents. And the people who are left . . . won't be . . . they won't be good. That's not how you survive, by being good . . . but—you all must be good and yet you made it this far." I want to ask him about the man outside, if he was good. "But you must be the exception."

He winces and leans forward a little, letting out a slow breath through his teeth and after a long moment, he straightens. His eyes are watery.

"Are you okay, Mr. Baxter?"

"Just tired," he assures me. "You all address me like I'm still your teacher."

"I'm sorry. We can—"

"I'm fine. I'm still your teacher . . ." He drums his fingers on the table. "If they hurt you, you can tell me. We can figure out what to do. You don't have to pretend that they're good."

It is so strange to hear this question from someone in this context. I think of all the times I sat in Baxter's class, long-sleeved sweaters on hot days, no one saying anything. I imagine how it would have sounded to me then. *If he hurt you, tell me. We can figure out what to do. You don't have to pretend that he's good.*

"I'm not. We went outside the night you got here," I say. "It didn't go well."

He stops drumming his fingers. "Why would you do something so ridiculous?"

I know I shouldn't say what I say next but I say it anyway.

"We went to get that man—the one you came here with." Baxter's face goes white but he doesn't say a word and I keep talking because I'm not smart but maybe these things should be said. "Mr. Baxter, we know you didn't come here alone. We know you came with another man—he was outside. He was calling for you when we got to him . . . he was calling your name. Nick. He was alive. He's not anymore. You can tell us about it. It's okay."

Baxter stares at me blankly. "I don't understand what you're saying. I came here alone."

My heart sinks. "You really can't remember how you got in?"

"You think I'd lie about that? Is that what you're telling me?"

I shake my head but when Cary and Rhys come back that's what I tell them. He's lying about everything.

In spite of this, I think most of us envision our future with Baxter as uncomfortable but inoffensive; the kind of situation where the other person is so strange, you start to wonder if the actual problem is you, so you don't say anything to them but nothing comes of it anyway and it's okay. I don't think any of us are expecting things to go so badly so quickly, but they do.

We are dead asleep when his shouting wakes us up.

"Where's the gun? *Where did you put the gun?* I want the gun—"

Baxter's voice echoes around the room, shrill and demanding. *The gun.* At first I think I'm dreaming but I realize my eyes are open and everyone is getting to their feet, so I do the same. Baxter stands at the edge of the stage with a flashlight, pushing aside garbage and crumpled clothes and running his hands through his hair.

"What the fuck?" Trace asks. "What's going on—"

Baxter turns to him. "Where did you put it?"

"Are they inside?" Harrison's as shrill as Baxter. "Did they get in—"

"No one got inside," Rhys says quickly. "Mr. Baxter—"

"*Where* is the *gun?*"

Cary steps forward. "Mr. B, what's wrong—"

"I want my gun, Mr. Chen. Where did you put it? I need it—"

"I don't have your gun. What do you need it for?"

Trace grabs the other flashlights and hands one to Grace. The room brightens. Baxter makes a frustrated noise and moves back to the stage, tries to climb up on it. Cary turns to Rhys, panicked, and I know right away the gun is somewhere beyond the curtain, somewhere obvious. Luckily, Baxter is too weak to get himself on the stage. He drops back to his feet.

"If Roger is out there, I need—"

Cary grabs Baxter by the arm and pulls him away.

"I think you're confused—"

"Roger is *out there!*" Baxter insists. He grabs at Cary's shirt, his eyes everywhere, unable to focus. "I need the gun. You have to understand. I *need* it—"

"I do—I understand—I totally understand—but we can't do anything until you calm down, okay? You need to calm down—"

"Roger is out there—"

"I know, but—"

"You have no idea what he'll do—"

"Mr. Baxter—"

"He's out there!"

"I know, but he's not *in here!*"

Finally, a combination of words that work. They sedate Baxter, make him go limp. He sinks to his knees and realizes where he is. The way he breathes is so ragged and so worn out.

"Harrison," Cary says. "Can you get Mr. Baxter some water?"

"I'm not going in the kitchen alone," Harrison says.

"I'll go with you," Trace says.

They are the only ones who move. The rest of us watch Baxter try to get a hold of himself. Cary's face is ashen. All of this is beyond him, beyond us. Grace moves to me. She grabs my hand and squeezes and just for a second, I feel the kind of strong she thinks I am.

Little gasps issue from Baxter's lips.

"I'm sorry," he tells Cary. "I'm sorry. I'm sorry. I'm so sorry. I don't know how to be comfortable, that's all. I don't—"

"It's okay."

"You have to understand—I've been outside so long—"

"We get it—"

"I don't know how to be comfortable."

"It's okay."

Cary helps Baxter to his feet. Baxter winces, falters a little, and rights himself at the same moment Trace and Harrison return with the water. Baxter takes it from them and presses the bottle against his sweaty forehead.

"I'm so sorry," he whispers.

"Who is Roger?" Rhys asks, because for some stupid reason he thinks this is the time to ask. I brace myself, expecting Baxter to go into another round of hysterics but thankfully, he doesn't. He flinches at someone else saying Roger's name, though. It's undeniable now, that something happened between them out there.

"I'd like to take a shower," Baxter says. "I need to—clear my head before we talk about this. Mr. Chen, maybe you could find me some clean clothes . . ."

"Sure," Cary says. Baxter nods, dazed. He drinks the water and then hands the half-full bottle to Trace. Cary hauls Mr. Baxter up by the arm. "Let's just . . . get you set up . . ."

We watch them exit the auditorium.

"If he's going to be like this the whole fucking time he's here," Trace says, "I don't know what I'm going to do."

"He's worse than Harrison," Rhys agrees. Harrison gives him an indignant look. Rhys ignores it and turns to me. "His name was Roger."

Roger. The man outside was Roger. Knowing his name makes it worse. I could have gone the rest of my life without knowing his name. My hands still feel what it was like to push him. If I think about it, I can hear him die, access that part of my memory easily. It makes me cold all over. The man outside, that I killed, was named Roger and Mr. Baxter knew him. I killed a man named Roger. My brain frantically tries to make excuses for me:

He was bad, he had to have been bad if Baxter left him out there, Baxter's scared of Roger enough to want to get the gun back, Roger was bad so it's good that I killed him . . .

"You should hide the gun somewhere else," I say to Rhys.

It's almost funny. Almost. The timing of my saying

that. Maybe later I'll think it was funny, we'll all think it was funny how the second it comes out of my mouth, Cary bursts into the room shouting, "I need the gun—*I need the gun!*"

Before we can react, he's onstage, past the curtain.

When he reappears, the gun is in his hand.

"What are you doing—"

"He's bitten—he's infected—"

Trace drops Baxter's water bottle and leaps away from it. "Holy shit—"

"Where?" Grace asks. "Where? I didn't see a bite—"

"His arm." Cary looks like he's going to vomit all over himself. "I got him some clothes from the drama room and when I got back he was getting undressed and I saw it. He didn't know I saw him but he's bitten. If he stays here, he turns and it doesn't matter how he got in because we're all dead anyway—"

Harrison covers his mouth. "Oh my God."

Cary stares at the gun and he looks so young, younger than Harrison, and then his face changes, becomes more resolved. He strides for the door.

"*Wait!*" Rhys grabs Cary by the arm and pulls him back. "You're going to kill him? You're going to go in there now and just fucking shoot him in the shower—"

"What else can we do?"

"Are you sure it's a bite?"

"*Yes!* It's—" Cary's throat hitches. He presses his hand against his mouth. When he's more sure of himself, he lowers it. "He'll turn."

"Is he hot? How does he feel?"

"*What?*"

"Like—like his temperature! Does he have a temperature? Is he cold?"

"He's fucking *bitten,* Rhys! There are *teeth marks* on his arm! I don't care how he *feels!*" Cary points to the hall with the gun and it looks like it belongs. A natural extension of his arm. "We have to get rid of him—"

"Are you *absolutely sure?* This is *not* the time to be wrong—"

"How many times do I have to—"

"Look, if you two pussies can't come to an agreement, just give me the fucking gun and I'll do it," Trace interrupts. "Or do you *want* to wait until he's turned?"

"What if he's turned *right now?*" Harrison asks.

Rhys sticks his fingers in his mouth and lets out a whistle loud and sharp enough to silence everyone. Even after we're quiet, he doesn't speak. We just stand there, staring at each other helplessly. And I think—at least with Roger, there was no time to think about it. This—there is time, enough of it. It's a decision so big it makes the room feel small and the only conclusion I can come to is we kill him, I think. He can't be in this school alive anymore. We can't keep him if he turns.

"He just got here," I say weakly, like it makes a difference. "He just got here. How do we tell him? Do we just tell him . . . ?"

Rhys shakes his head. "Don't—"

"You have to do it fast." I'm babbling but I can't stop.

"Maybe it's dark enough that he won't see, so you have to do it fast and you have to do it—you have to do it right . . . so you have to get him in the head—"

"Sloane—"

"And then—his body. We can't keep it—"

"Sloane, *stop*," Rhys begs. "We don't even know if he's really bitten."

Cary turns to him, mouth open. "I just told you he was."

"Even if he's not, he's clearly unstable," Trace points out. "And he woke up freaking for his *gun*. What happens if he finds it the next time and accidentally shoots one of us?"

"He's lying to us about not remembering how he got in and he lied to Sloane about being out there alone," Cary says. "He's not acting normal—"

"What the fuck is *normal*?" Rhys demands. "So he freaked out a little and he lied—these are *not* good enough reasons to end someone's life!"

"You want to kill me?"

My insides disappear. Baxter stands in the doorway. His hair is wet, flattened against his head, and he's in fresh clothes, dress pants on, a new shirt. He walks into the room looking more our teacher than he ever has—but his eyes are so sad, so disappointed in us.

"You're infected," Cary says.

"What? What are you talking about? I didn't—"

"Your arm. I saw it."

Baxter shakes his head slowly. He steps forward and the rest of us take a collective step back and I know at that moment this is settled. Even if we spend the next hour letting Baxter try to negotiate his own survival, we have already decided he's going to die.

"Can I see it?" Rhys asks. "The bite?"

Baxter studies us. I'm hoping for something but I don't know what it is. I want him to handle it the right way. I want him to make it easier on all of us. In a way, he does.

He does the most condemnable thing ever.

He tries to run.

"Get him!" Trace shouts. He actually shouts that.

The world comes down on Baxter. Rhys, Cary, and Trace have him on the floor and the gun skitters beyond them. I grab it while Cary and Trace hold Baxter down and Rhys asks Cary, "Which arm? *Which arm?*"

Cary says, "Left! It's the left—"

Rhys rolls up Baxter's shirtsleeve. Grace shines the light on it. I've never seen a bite close up. It's raw and angry, red and yellow teeth marks. The skin is clean—thanks to the shower—but inflamed. Weeping, sore. It looks like a fever.

"It's not what you think. I promise, it's not—"

Rhys presses his hand against Baxter's forehead.

"If it's not a bite, what is it?" Rhys asks. "You have to tell us what it is."

"It's—it's not—" We wait. Baxter's face crumples. "It's a bite." Harrison runs to the farthest corner of the room. "*No*—it's not—it's a bite—but it's not—you have to listen to me—it's not from one of *them*—I promise you—"

"But it's infected," Grace whispers. "Look at it—"

"*I'm not infected!* I'm not—you *have* to believe me, *I'm not*—"

"You have a bite but it's not from the infected?" Trace asks incredulously. "That's what you want us to believe?"

"That's what it *is*!"

"Bullshit! You're just saying that because you don't want to die—"

"I think he's telling the truth," Rhys says.

But I'm the only one who hears him say it and I don't have the courage to ask him to repeat himself. I look at Baxter's arm, the bite, and I don't understand how Baxter could be telling the truth. He's infected and he needs to die.

"Who has the gun?" Cary asks. "Who has it?"

"Sloane," Grace says.

Me. I have it. The gun. I stare at it. It's heavy in my hands, hot. I raise it, feeling equal parts absurd and terrified out of my mind. I point it at Baxter. This is what they want me to do, isn't it? This is what has to be done. Baxter starts to shout, but I can't tell what he's saying. It has the lilt of a prayer, though. I close my eyes.

"*No!*" Rhys shouts. "Jesus, Sloane, no—"

I imagine the gun going off. A hole between Baxter's eyes. It's so real to me, I start to shake. Hands around my hands. Rhys gently takes the gun from me and I feel like I'm turning into nothing and I don't know if it's because he is taking the gun out of my hands or because the gun was in them.

"I didn't know what you wanted me to do," I say faintly.

"Shoot him!" Trace. "Just fucking do it—"

"I want to put it to a vote," Rhys says. "We have to make this *fair*—"

"You're going to be outnumbered," Cary tells him. "No matter what."

"We don't have to kill him—"

"What else are we going to *do*?"

"If I leave," Baxter says over us, "you'll never know how I got in."

And then he starts to cry.

We're not murderers.

We are still good people and this was the choice we were forced to make. Baxter has to leave or he has to die. The evidence is damning. He's bitten. He's unstable. He's lied to us.

That's more than enough, especially now.

We're in the library. The flashlights are set on the table, aimed at us like a crude spotlight. Baxter is in front of the door, the way out, preparing himself for whatever is next. I think of Rhys and me, standing in that exact spot just days before and how much has changed in that time. Harrison and Grace hover by some shelves. Trace and Cary clear the barricades away and then they're gone. Two things have to happen next: someone has to open the door and Baxter has to step through it. But what happens after that? He lives until the infection overtakes him? We go on, like nothing happened? Because nothing happened if no one used the gun, right? Still, Baxter's outcome is inevitable. He is going to die.

But we're not murderers.

Even though Rhys has the gun aimed directly at Baxter's head.

It will only be used if Baxter is uncooperative and insists on jeopardizing us.

"If you try to get in again, however you got in before," Cary says, "we'll have to kill you."

"You, Mr. Chen? You'll do it?"

"*I'll* do it," Trace mutters.

"I'm so sorry, Mr. Baxter," Rhys says, and he sounds like he means it and it makes me feel like maybe there's a chance we're doing something really wrong here. "You have to realize—"

"You'll never find it," Baxter interrupts. "How I got in."

"We will."

Baxter looks at his hands. "I'm not infected, though. I was not bitten by an infected."

He's been saying this since we came to our decision. It's like if he sounds plaintive enough, we'll let him stay. If that was all we needed from him, I know we'd let him stay. I know we're not bad people, not deep down inside.

"No one knows what I've been through," he whispers.

He turns to us and I take a step back. I don't want to look at him, don't want his empty eyes and his hollowed-out face etched in my memory. Baxter turns to Cary.

"You were never a very good student. I couldn't make you do anything," he says, and Cary doesn't argue this, just nods. Baxter sighs and closes his eyes. "Maybe, though, you'd be the one to open the door."

"Okay," Cary says.

He crosses in front of Baxter to do it.

Baxter charges at Cary faster than any of us can blink. I immediately see how we've done everything wrong. We thought we were stronger, smarter than a man who spent weeks out there on his own and lived this long. Cary doesn't even have time to make a sound. They fall and his head collides with the door, leaving him dazed and limp enough for Baxter to grab Cary's arm and I know what's going to happen before it happens and there's nothing I can do to stop it. Baxter sinks his teeth into Cary's arm.

Cary comes back to himself then, screams like I've never heard anyone scream before. I glimpse red and a thousand more things happen at once. Trace rips the gun out of Rhys's hands and shouts for him to *open the fucking door! Get him out of here!* Rhys springs into action, heaving Baxter up by the shoulders and the whole time he does it, Baxter is still trying to make a case for himself. His teeth are stained with Cary's blood.

"I'm not infected! You'll see—*I'm not infected!*"

"Someone *help me!*" Rhys fights Baxter to the door. "Help me—"

I do it. I push the door open and the cold air calls to me. I want to step ahead of them both, but there's a flurry of movement and Baxter's flailing arm hits me in the chest, forcing me back. Rhys shoves him once. Hard.

Baxter is gone.

The door closes. It's quiet just for a second and then his fists sound desperately against it.

Let me in.

Let me in.

Let me in.

And then it stops.

"Get the barricade back up," Rhys says. "Now—"

"Wait," Trace says.

"What?"

"*Wait.*" Trace trains the gun on Cary, who is staring at his bloody, bitten arm. "Cary's been bitten. Doesn't he have to go outside too?"

Cary looks up. "No—I didn't—it's not—"

"We all saw it, Chen. You're bitten."

"*Trace,*" Rhys says.

Trace ignores him. His eyes stay fixed on Cary.

"Trace," I say. "Think about what you're saying—"

"But *why?* That's what we just did to Baxter. Baxter's infected. Baxter bit Cary. Cary is infected. It's simple. Anything that risks me or Grace is not allowed to stay in this fucking building. Chen, tell me which way you want to leave."

Cary's face loses all color. He holds his arm out and

blood trails down it, drips onto his shirt. He silently begs Trace for his life. Trace winces, but the gun stays aimed at Cary's face. It is so ugly.

"I brought us here," Cary whispers.

"Doesn't matter. Baxter bit you and now you're infected."

"Give me the gun, Trace," Rhys says.

"Back the *fuck off,* Moreno."

"Come on. We can quarantine him until he turns. The nurse's office."

"We didn't do that for Baxter. Why should we do that for Chen? After what he did to my parents? Give me one good reason why."

"Because Rhys is right."

Her voice shocks us, makes us quiet. Trace's grip on the gun nearly falters. We all turn to her. Grace stands there, nervous but determined. She moves to Trace and puts her hand on his arm. He swallows hard and I think maybe he's as scared at the idea of killing Cary as we are. But that doesn't really mean anything as long as he still has the gun.

"Don't even," he tells her.

"They're dead. It's not going to change. Hey, look at me," she says. Trace refuses to. He leaves her no option but to stand directly between him and Cary. The way she moves is almost holy; Cary stares at her like she's a saint. And Trace—as soon as she's in front of him, he lowers the gun and I can tell that even the millisecond he had it pointed at her has hurt him, scarred him. "They wouldn't want you to do this."

"Grace. He. Is. Bitten."

"But he hasn't turned. If he turns—"

"He can do whatever he wants to me," Cary says. He clutches his arm to his chest and I think—*Cary's going to die before me.* We'll lose Cary.

"Trace," Grace pleads.

I stagger out of the library because I can't listen to them talk about Cary's fate like he's not in the room, can't listen to how he's going to die before me. When I hit the hall, I run. I run upstairs, past the second floor, to the third floor. I rip the posterboard down and I stare out at Cortege below. The moon is bright enough to illuminate the street, but I don't see Baxter and I think about how this day must have been carved out for him from the moment he was born, that he would live, find Madeline, teach high school, meet Roger, and end up in here with us, his death.

PART THREE

Cary won't talk.

He lays on the cot while Rhys douses the bite in peroxide. It bubbles angrily and he doesn't even flinch. Rhys dabs away the blood with a wet cloth until the wound is clean. Then salve. I can't get over the damage, what human teeth can do. What Baxter's teeth have done. It shouldn't surprise me after everything we've seen, but it does. An actual piece of Cary's arm is missing and that part of

Cary's arm was in Baxter's mouth. I try to remember if he spit it out, but I can't and then I think I'll be sick.

"I don't think you're infected," Rhys tells Cary as he bandages Cary's arm. Cary doesn't respond. "Cary, you're not going to die. I mean, you're not going to die from this."

Cary grimaces and presses his face into his pillow. Rhys finishes with the bandages and Cary clutches his arm to his chest. He shivers. Rhys frowns and feels Cary's forehead, just for a second. Three days. We are giving Cary three days. We figure if he hasn't turned by then, he won't. But I don't think anyone believes he won't. Three days.

In three days, it will be twenty-five days since the world ended.

Eighteen spent in this school.

It feels like years.

"Someone will bring you food. We'll check on you by the hour. Cary." Rhys waits for Cary to acknowledge him. He doesn't. "Cary, if you're still you three days from now, you're going to be fine. So don't do anything stupid, okay?"

Cary doesn't say anything and I want to draw the blankets up around his shoulders, a gesture of comfort, but most of me is afraid to touch him. Rhys and I stand there and listen to him breathe and I wonder if Cary feels how sick people feel when they're told they're terminal, that their time on earth is going to be so much less than they thought. He must. This is the day that was carved out for him.

"Cary," Rhys says.

Cary still doesn't respond. Rhys stands there. I can tell

he wants to do more but there's nothing else he can do. We leave the nurse's office. He locks the door behind him. I hate him for that, hate him for telling Cary he's not infected and then turning around and locking that door. I'm about to tell him so when Grace appears.

"What do you want, Grace?" Rhys asks.

"How is he?"

"Well, let's see—he's been bitten and had a gun pointed at his face all in the span of like an hour. How do you think he is?"

"Can I see him?" she asks. Rhys sighs. "I mean alone. Not with you."

"What do you want to see him for?"

"Doesn't matter," she says. "I saved him."

He snorts. I'm amazed. I don't know how she can say or do things like this and call *me* the strong one. She holds out her hand. Rhys doesn't give her the keys right away. He stares at them for a long time, and when he finally hands them over, he's clearly not happy about it.

"Thank you," she says.

"Bring them straight back to me," he says. Grace nods and moves to the door. "And Grace?" She pauses. "If I find out Trace is bothering Cary—shooting his mouth, threatening him, or just hanging around, whatever—I will beat the shit out of him. Okay?"

Grace's face turns a furious shade of red but she wants to keep the keys more than she wants to borrow trouble, so she just nods. I want to watch her go to Cary but Rhys tugs on my hand. We walk down the hall. My back is to the nurse's office when its door opens and closes. Rhys and I are quiet. It's going to be weird to come back to the auditorium, just to Trace and Harrison.

"If you think he's not infected, then why did you lock the door?" I ask.

"Because I'm the only one who thinks he's not."

"Why do you think that?"

"I'm an optimist, I guess."

"Don't bullshit me. Why do you think that?" He quickens his pace, trying to get away from me, but I stand in front of him. "You said that about Baxter too. Tell me how you know." He clenches his jaw. "Rhys."

"They were both bitten but they're not . . . cold," he says.

"What does that mean?"

"Baxter was bitten before he got here and he'd been in here for a couple of days. When people get bitten, they get cold. How fast it happens depends on the bite. If he was infected, he would've already been cold."

"How do you know that?"

He looks away. "Doesn't matter. Maybe I'm wrong. Maybe it's different now, I don't know. Maybe they don't get cold anymore. But if Cary doesn't turn in the next forty-eight hours, I don't think he's going to."

"So you knew Baxter wasn't infected and you let him go out there to die."

"Are you kidding me? I got him out of this school *alive*."

"But you didn't say about the bites—you *knew* and you let them—"

"And *you* held the fucking gun in his face! You were ready to kill him!"

I hate when people yell at me. Hate it. There's been so much shouting lately, it's hard to be totally bothered by it now, but this—this is *at* me. I storm down the hall, but he keeps pace with me and then he cuts me off before I can step inside the auditorium. Harrison's and Trace's voices drift into the hall and they sound normal. It makes everything worse.

"You had the gun on him too," I whisper.

"I know," he says. "It doesn't matter if he was infected or not. He lied to us and no one wanted him here. No one would have believed me about the bites if I'd said it and I already put my ass on the line for Cary. Look—hey, look at me." I look at him. "That whole thing happened way too fast. Okay?"

I swallow. "Okay."

We step inside the auditorium. When Grace comes back, Trace rounds on her.

"What were you doing in there with him?"

"Don't start."

"What the *fuck* were you doing in there with him *alone*? Are you out of your *mind*?"

"I just wanted to talk to him—"

"There's nothing you need to say to Cary Chen and if there is, it's not going to matter soon anyway. Stay away from him, Gracie. I'm not kidding."

"He hasn't turned," she says.

"Yeah, well, I'm counting the days till he does. Dibs on braining him—"

"Shut the fuck up, Trace," Rhys says, "or I'll shut you up."

"Try."

Rhys moves forward and then he stops. They stare at each other and a smile slowly stretches across Trace's face.

"Where did you put the gun?" Rhys asks.

"Somewhere safe."

"Tell me where you put it."

"No."

Rhys looks a second away from exploding, jumping Trace, something. Trace senses it. His smile vanishes at the same time Rhys recovers. It's the most incredible show of restraint.

"Why not?" Rhys asks. "I went out there for your dad. I thought we were cool."

"That was then," Trace replies. "I don't like how you put Baxter before us. I don't like how you or Price there put Chen before us. I don't think you should have the gun."

"But—"

"That's fair," Harrison says, surprising us.

"I didn't say it wasn't," Rhys says slowly. "But what happens to it after Cary comes back?"

"He's not coming back," Trace says.

"If he hasn't turned in three days, he's not turning. And we're a group," Rhys says. "We should decide this stuff as a group—"

"Sure, whatever you say." Trace shrugs. "Whoever thinks I should keep the gun until after this thing with Chen is resolved, raise your hand."

Three hands go up. Trace, Grace, and Harrison.

"Okay," Rhys says. He holds his hand out to Trace.

Trace hesitates and then they shake.

I don't believe in either of them.

Rhys visits Cary every hour. Sometimes I want to go with him, but I can't bring myself to do it. I keep thinking of how we sent Baxter out, him pounding against the door. The only thing that manages to pull me out of my thoughts are Grace and Trace. They argue quietly in the corner. I know it's about Cary. Grace's arms are crossed. Trace actually points at her like he's her father and then she snaps something at him. They stand there for a minute, then he gives her this hug and it's over, I guess, even if it's not resolved. Is this how brothers and sisters fight? It's not the way Lily and I ever fought.

Grace wanders over to me. I ask her what she said to Cary, what Trace said to her, but she won't tell me and my prying sends her away. She flops down on one of the couches and eventually, I go to sleep. Morning has crept up on us, but it doesn't matter. When I wake up again, it's still day. The auditorium is uncomfortably quiet. A quick look around the room tells me Grace, Harrison, and Trace are gone. At my left is Rhys. He's asleep, one arm splayed out, half on his mat, half off it. His hand rests on the floor, open. I get this urge I can't resist. I reach over and gently press my index finger into his palm.

He doesn't wake up. I do it again, let it stay there for the longest time and he's too asleep to feel it. I stare at his face. His lips are parted slightly. His breathing is rhythmic, even. His shirt has ridden up past his abdomen.

LaVallee's keys are clipped to his belt loop.

I want to see Cary. I don't want to ask Rhys's permission. I watch him for a little longer, gathering courage and when I have it, I sit up and move close to him, as close as I can get to him. My hands are at his jeans, trying to unhook the keys. This is not how I imagined the first time I'd fumble with some guy's pants would go.

Rhys grabs my wrist and stares at me through half-lidded eyes.

"What are you doing?" he asks thickly.

"I want to see Cary."

His eyes drift shut. He swallows.

"Just give me a minute." He sounds distant. "We'll go and see Cary . . ."

I wait, but he doesn't move. He's fallen back asleep and I'm glad because I want to see Cary alone. In one quick motion, I unclip the keys and hurry out of the auditorium. I don't see Trace, Grace, or Harrison on my way to the nurse's office and maybe I should worry about that, but I don't because if anyone's fine it's them.

Cary is on his cot when I unlock the door and I think maybe I should have brought him something to eat or drink. But then I notice a tray of uneaten food on the nearby desk. Cary looks at me but he doesn't speak.

"If you were expecting Rhys, he's sleeping," I say.

"Not surprised. He took a metric shit-ton of Benadryl the last time he was in here."

I sit beside him, reach over, and press both of my hands against his face. He's not cold. If anything, he's hot. Cary wraps his hands around my wrist and gently lowers them.

"Did Rhys tell you about the—"

"Yes."

THIS IS NOT A TEST

"So you're not infected," I say. He shrugs. "I thought you'd be happy."

"You saw how quick they were going to throw me out of here."

"It was just Trace."

"I really thought I was bitten, Sloane. I thought that was it for me."

"It's not."

"Makes you think, though. The apocalypse: one big existential crisis." He cracks a smile. "But whatever, right? I'm here, I'm alive, probably not infected. Great."

"What did Grace say to you when she was in here?"

"That's between me and her," he says. "But I didn't tell her what Rhys said about the bites. I don't know if he told you but he doesn't want them to know what he knows. He's pissed at them."

Neither of us says anything. It's nice to be able to sit with someone and not say anything. Something about it makes me brave. It makes me do something I don't entirely understand. I lean over and wrap my arms around Cary. I rest my head against his chest. He tenses but then he wraps his arms around me. I don't feel anything about Cary that's romantic.

I just want this.

"I loved your sister," he says.

It's so unexpected, it's beyond processing. And then, as it slowly sinks in, I look up at him.

"But I Never . . . you said—"

"What, you think I'm going to put all my cards on the

table? I knew you were freaked when I told you we had sex."
He sighs. "It was that unrequited bullshit, anyway . . . she
didn't know. Never knew. Now I can't stop thinking about
it. Maybe telling you is the closest I'll get."

"Why didn't you tell her?"

"Lily had to keep me at an arm's length to have sex with
me. She didn't like to get personal, so I didn't."

"You really think she made it?"

Cary lets the question hang in the air. The last time we
talked about her, he said she'd make it but when we played
I Never, he also said he'd never been in love.

"I hope she did. I like to think she did."

"She left me," I say. "She didn't tell me she was going."

"She had things to figure out."

"I thought you said you never got personal."

"It didn't get personal enough."

"What do you think she had to figure out?"

"I don't know. She said she felt hopeless once," he says.
He pauses. "Trapped. She never felt free. I thought it was
one of those post-high-school I-have-no-idea-what-I-want-
to-do-with-my-life meltdowns. Was it?"

Letting this conversation happen was like putting a toe
in the ocean and now the water is over my head. The way
we hold each other changes, in that I stop. My whole body
turns to stone. It doesn't escape his notice. I sense my name
on the tip of his tongue, but I don't give him the opportu-
nity to say it. I get to my feet but as soon as we're not
touching, I feel it so much.

"I should get back to the auditorium before they start
wondering," I say.

"What you should really be doing is looking for Baxter's way in," he says, and he's right. That's what I should be doing. That's what all of us should be doing. "Don't forget to lock the door on your way out."

I do and then I just stand there in the hall.

What she told me: it was us two, nobody else. Our future was our freedom. She was the one who tied and knotted us together, made escape with her the only thing I wanted, convinced me there was nothing else to want.

But I knew she hated it.

I can't do this anymore, I'm so sorry.

Just because she said it to Cary first—

I wrap my arms around myself and circle the school. Trace's, Harrison's, and Grace's voices sound from the gym. When I step inside, the basketball is in Harrison's hands and everything about this moment is something I want to kill.

"We should be looking for how Baxter got in," I say.

"Don't start," Trace says. "Already got this lecture from Moreno."

"Yeah, for good reason. It's important we find it."

"So important he's all hopped up on Benadryl and passed out in the auditorium, right? Hey, have you seen Cary? Has he turned? Let me know as soon as it happens."

I guess the sparkle of how I went outside for him has faded, all for not wanting him to kill Cary, for voting against him about the gun. I head back into the hall.

Baxter's way in is also a way out.

If I find it, I can leave.

I comb classrooms and closets, push against walls

absurdly, like they might move. I cannot find it. I go back to the auditorium. Rhys is still in a coma. I hook the keys back onto his jeans and then, impulsively, press my hand against his face. He stirs a little. Leans into my palm. I run my fingers over his skin for the longest time and he never wakes up.

Hopeless.

Grace insists on taking Cary breakfast.

"No way." Trace tries to take the tray from her hands.

"I wasn't asking you," she says. "I'm telling you."

"No," Trace says slowly. "*I'm* telling *you.* I don't want you anywhere near him when he's like this. Stop being stupid, Grace."

"Last I checked him—like an hour ago—he was fine,"

Rhys says. "I doubt anything is going to happen to her if she goes in there right now."

"Moreno can give Chen his breakfast," Trace says. "Why are you doing this?"

"As student government president, I had to deal with people I didn't like all the time," she snaps. "I had to listen to them and then I had to advocate for them if they needed it—"

"News flash: you're not student government president anymore."

"And you're not the boss of me!" Trace laughs at how childish she sounds and that makes her angrier. When he sees the look on her face, he stops laughing.

"Grace." He's full-on patronizing now. "Don't be like this—"

"I told you we had to let it go." She raises her trembling chin. "This is me letting it go."

Something in her face tells him he's not going to win this. He steps aside and Grace hurries out of the room and Trace glares after her and then transfers that glare to me, to Rhys.

"I put the gun down," he says. "That's as much as I'm letting it go."

"You're a great man, Trace," Rhys says.

Trace shoots Rhys a dirty look and then heads out of the auditorium. A second later, he pokes his head back in and calls for Harrison. Harrison actually goes running to him.

I stare after them. "How did that even happen?"

"Trace has the gun," Rhys says. "Harrison has joined his army."

"This isn't war."

"Maybe we can convince Grace to become a double agent or something," Rhys says thoughtfully. He catches my eye and laughs a little at the ridiculousness of what he's just said and then he looks away. "She's got the right idea, though. Grace."

"What's that?"

"That this isn't a good time or place to hold on to things."

I think I know what he's going to say next and I don't think I want to hear it, so I get to my feet, searching for some excuse to leave the room.

But Rhys says, "Sloane," before I can find one.

"What?"

"I don't want . . ." he trails off, and tries to figure out a way to put it. "I don't want how I feel about you to get in the way." I don't say anything, just leave him hanging, which is cruel. "I mean I don't want to hate you so much that—I'm like how Trace is with Cary because that's going to fuck him over in the end. I want to forget about what happened outside."

He keeps waiting for me to say something.

"I forgive you," he says.

"Okay."

"That's all you have to say?"

"What do you want me to say?"

"Thank you?"

"I didn't ask you to forgive me."

Rhys stares at the ceiling for a second and then he leaves the auditorium and since I have the room to myself,

I go back to sleep until a slow roll of thunder wakes me up. By the time my eyes are open, a loud clap of it sounds over-head.

And then the rain, tapping against the skylights.

I am so sad.

I am so sad it makes me heavier than the sum of my parts. I shift, restless, but it doesn't help. It's like—time. All this time in here is on me, has its hooks in me. Maybe if I sleep more, I'll wake up and I'll feel different, but I can't. The storm is really happening now and it makes the room feel emptier. Makes me feel emptier.

I get up. I want to see Cary. I want to talk to him about Lily again. I need him to make everything he told me about her hurt less somehow. The walk to him takes forever. It's hard to breathe around how badly I feel right now. I round the corner and when the nurse's office comes into sight, I'm grateful.

And then I remember I don't have the key.

And then I want to break things.

But—the door is open. A little.

It stops me cold. Not right. That's not right. I back up, think about finding Rhys, but there might not be time. I tiptoe over cautiously.

Grace's voice.

"Stop talking, stop talking," she's saying over Cary, who is mumbling something at her. "Just stop talking. Shut up. Stop. Stop. Talking—"

Their voices cut off abruptly. I step into the room and peer around the door, past the desk and supply cabinets and posters about knowing your body.

The cot is empty and they're beside it.

Cary has Grace up against the wall.

Cary has Grace pressed against the wall.

I process this like a two-year-old with no life beyond Disney movies: *he's hurting her.* Then I realize, no—not hurting.

Kissing.

Cary and Grace.

I feel a little Norman Bates standing there, watching it happen between them. The way their hands fumble and grope all over each other, the way he kisses her mouth and her throat and how when he kisses her throat she leans her head back, all the way back, like nothing feels better than his lips against her skin. And then she lowers her head. She puts her palms against his face and makes him look at her and my throat tightens for what's in her eyes. I don't think she forgives him but it's like her heart is a little more open than it was.

It would be so easy for them to catch me spying, but they can only see each other. Grace kisses Cary and suddenly everything is just slow and tender in a way it wasn't before. The energy in the room shifts. They're kissing still, but now they're *really* kissing. It's so open and so honest and so end-of-the-world and I can feel it from where I'm standing. I feel the absence of it from where I'm standing. I don't know how much longer I can go on like this.

Still here. Still here. Still here.

Cary and Grace.

I hear them breathing.

I move away from the scene slowly and then I'm in the

hall, tears in my eyes. I run past LaVallee's office, past the auditorium where Trace and Harrison's voices now float out. I push through the doors to the gym and Rhys is there, smoking. The first thing I want to say is *Cary and Grace have paired off* but I can't because it will make the thing I'm about to do worse, wrong. I calm down. Walk across the gym slowly.

"What's wrong?" he asks.

I bite my lip and turn my head in the direction of the hall. He grinds the cigarette out and follows me out. I don't look back at him.

I pick the locker rooms because they're closest.

Once we're inside he says, "Is it Cary?"

I shake my head.

"What is it?"

"Thank you," I tell him.

"Whatever," he says.

I should ask permission first, but I can't. I move to him and then—I press him against the wall. My hands fumble and grope all over him and he lets it happen. His mouth is just as hungry against mine. He tastes lonely. I feel it all through him. It's what's making him not stop this, not ask questions, it makes him kiss me back. He was with girls all the time. They were always around him. I bet he hasn't been used to not having anyone to touch like this and I've never—I've never had that.

And that makes me so angry I don't know if I want to hurt him for it, for having it. Hurt Lily for having it. I kiss his throat hard, clumsily. I want him to feel it. I want to feel this. I need it to hurt for me to feel it, I think.

206

I run my hands all over him, dig my nails into his skin, and he says, "Sloane—"

And I look him in the eyes and he has the most incredible eyes. They're unremarkable—a muddy brown—but they show me he's as empty as I am.

He kisses me and his lips are soft. I don't want soft lips. I want to feel it. He puts his hands on my waist and turns me around so I'm the one against the wall. In that brief moment, I take in the room around us. There's barely any light in here. The storm is still outside. The rain, I hear it. I imagine it. Fat drops of water splashing onto roofs, tracing slick wet trails down before turning back into smaller droplets that hit the pavement and splash, making puddles.

"Your shirt," Rhys mumbles.

My fingers unbutton my buttons. Nine buttons until my shirt is open. He slides it off my shoulders and it hangs from my elbows. He steps back a little, looks at me. I'm not wearing a bra, but then I remember he's seen this before. He brings his palm against my skin, against my collarbone. He's shaking and I'm dizzy. He kisses me again, hard. Finally.

The sky cracks open, thunder, and then all I can think about is the rain, the smell of the pavement after it rains. That musty beautiful smell that coats your lungs. A mild spring day, two girls in blue raincoats with yellow buttons shaped like flowers. Lily taking off her boots, grabbing my hands, and trying to drag me through all the puddles she could. I was always too scared and—she always let go of my hand.

"Sloane?"

Rhys's voice brings me back, pulls me out of the memory. My hand disappears from Lily's hand, the puddles disappear under my feet and it's just me and him, but it's not really me and him. It's just this emptiness between us, the stupid idea I could kiss it away, and I'm crying before I can stop myself and then we're on the floor and his arms are all around me and I keep saying *I can't* because I don't know what else to say. He tries to calm me, quiet me. Brings his hand to my face, tells me it's okay. It's not okay. I'm dying. I am dying. I have finally achieved what I set out to do. My heart is splitting open and I breathe in but no air gets into my lungs. I push against Rhys but he won't let me go, so I lean into him, curl my fingers into his shirt and sob and the only thing that makes me feel okay about it is the fact that Cary broke down before me, Grace, she broke down before me, Harrison. But still, every second like this hurts, it hurts so bad I can't stand it. I want it to stop, that's all I've wanted. I let go of Rhys's shirt when my fingers start to ache. I let him go, but his hold on me never wavers and it is so quiet.

And then he asks, "Why can't you?"

The floor in the locker rooms is cold.

The floor is cold and Rhys is warm.

"Because she couldn't." I say it so quietly, he has to rest his head against mine to hear me. "She told me she couldn't do it anymore."

"Do what?"

"Be my sister."

These words cut me, feel like they cut me when they

come out. They tear up my lips, make them bleed. I'm your sister, Lily. I never stopped being your sister.

"Why?"

"Because—our dad beat us. We were going to leave together. We had this plan but she left me with him instead because being stuck with me made her feel trapped . . . she left me and—" I think of myself sitting on the edge of the bathtub and it was so long ago, too long, and I start to cry again. "I've been here so much longer than I was supposed to be—"

He tells me it's going to be okay until all the words blur together into a hum that makes me close my eyes and I start to go away and five, ten, fifteen minutes later, I'm aware of my hand sliding down to his lap and then nothingness and then the gentle sensation of his index finger pressing into my open palm and then his hand is at my face, running his fingers across my skin and I'm so awake. I untangle myself from his grasp and get to my feet so fast it surprises him. I can't look him in the eyes. Rhys grabs my hand and tries to pull me back down but I jerk away.

"Sloane, wait—"

My shirt is still undone, wide open. My face burns. I button it up so hastily, every button is one button off. I have to get out of here. I push out of the locker room and run. His voice chases me down the halls. I duck into the girls' room and lock myself in a stall and then I just sit there with my head against the side of it. I don't even realize I'm not alone until I hear my name and then I freeze and lift my feet off the ground, like this could make me invisible.

"Sloane?" Grace pushes against the stall door. The lock rattles. "I know you're in there. I saw you run in. What's wrong?" I press my lips together. "Sloane." The lock rattles again. "Open the door."

I reach forward and unlock it. Grace steps back.

"I saw you with Cary," I say.

"What—" She stops. "That's why you're upset?"

I leave the stall, push past her. "So the last few weeks were just a total game to you? You just—you and Trace make it hell to be in here, you push Cary until he's broken and then we all have to pick sides but then you're basically *fucking* him in the nurse's office—"

"Sloane—"

"That is *not* cool, Grace!" I want to break something. I storm toward the door and then double back. She stares at me, her mouth hanging open. "Give me the keys."

"What?"

"Give me the keys to the nurse's office."

"Why?"

"I want to see Cary. Give me the keys or I'll tell Trace what you were doing—"

"What is your problem? I came in here because I heard you *crying* and I wanted to see if I could help—" I hold my hand out, cutting her off. She looks at me and she knows I am not going to talk about this with her anymore. She digs into her pockets and gives me the keys along with a pleading look. "Please don't tell Trace about this."

I promise her nothing. I go back to the nurse's office. My hands are shaking so badly it takes me forever to unlock the door, so it's not like I surprise Cary or anything.

He's laying on the cot and I think he looks satisfied. I hate him. I slam the door behind me.

"I thought you loved my sister."

He sits up. "What—"

"I saw you with Grace. I thought you loved my sister."

He has to separate the sentences before he can tackle either of them.

"Sloane—"

"I saw you with Grace."

"Sloane—"

"And you were wrong about her anyway," I say. He gets up and steps toward me and I step back. I wish I had a switch, some way I could turn myself off. And now I'm just lying, I don't know why I'm lying. I'm lying because I'm the only one that can say the things I need to hear. "You were wrong about Lily. You were wrong about her. I'm her sister. I would know. She was—she wasn't like—she was free. She wasn't trapped—"

"Okay, but—"

"You were *wrong*—"

"Sloane—"

Cary stops. His gaze catches something behind me. I turn. Rhys stands in the doorway, staring at us. I shove the keys in his hands and leave them both standing there and all I can think is how she left me when I needed her and that I need her. I still need her.

I sleep. I refuse to be awake. In the afternoon, Trace asks Rhys if I'm sick. I open my eyes and ask him if he'll shoot me depending on my answer, which goes over about as well as I expect it to.

"Sloane, get up," Rhys says at one point. "Move around."

I stare at the skylight. It's raining again. A rainy spring that will turn into what kind of summer? It's hard to imagine it summer, everything bright and alive and someone,

213

somewhere not having sorted all of this end-of-the-world stuff out.

I go back to sleep.

Eventually, Rhys prods me awake and volunteers me to take Cary his dinner and I don't want to but he says I have to, that he won't leave me alone until I do. Grace, mysteriously, has given up the job. I grudgingly take a tray down to the nurse's office. Cary is not surprised to see me. I set the food on the desk without looking at him and head for the door.

"She never took her shirt off," he says at my back. I stop. "When we were together. I thought it was cute because she was usually so confident. I never thought she was hiding something."

I see them in my head. They're in a car, the backseat, they're all over each other. He's trying to push her shirt up, she's pulling it back down and playing coy to hide the bruises.

I turn. "Rhys shouldn't have told you."

"Maybe but you need to bury it," Cary tells me. "All of that's over. You have to be here now."

Bury it. Lily is gone, has been gone. It's been weeks since I had to face my father and the last of those bruises have been replaced by ones that have nothing to do with him. I don't want to be here now. Especially now.

"You're not infected," I say. Cary nods and looks at his still-bandaged arm. "Which means Baxter wasn't infected, which means we let him go outside to die. Does it bother you?"

"I'm just glad it wasn't me."

"What about the Caspers?" I ask. "Are you glad that wasn't you now? Did Grace forgive you? What about that?"

"I'm as close as I'm getting."

"So you buried it," I say. "You're here now."

"Yeah."

"Enjoy your dinner, Cary."

I leave, locking the door behind me. I make it a short way down the hall before I stop and lean against the wall, my head buzzing, trying to figure out everything Cary knows. Rhys told him about me and Lily. Did Rhys tell him I wanted to die? Did Rhys tell Cary what we did? When Cary sees me, does he see a girl with her shirt open, pressed up against Rhys?

I go to the bathroom and I check my forehead. Underneath the bandage, my skin is raw pink and red, gouged out and trying desperately to heal. I'll have to change the bandage soon, but all of the first aid is with Cary and I don't want to see him again. I leave the bathroom and make my way to the auditorium. I'm almost there when Rhys charges out of it. He shouts my name.

"Sloane, I need the key to the nurse's office—we have to get Cary."

Figures.

"What's wrong?" I ask.

"Nothing. We just have to get him now."

He won't tell me what it's about before we get to Cary. He won't even tell me after we get to Cary, just says we have to get back to the auditorium now, it's important. There's a strange energy about him, not dire, but urgent. When we step inside the room, Grace, Trace, and Harrison are huddled around the radio. Trace turns it off as soon as he spots Cary.

"What is he doing out? It's not tomorrow yet—"

"Cut the bullshit, Trace," Rhys says. "You know he's not infected—"

"We agreed on three days. Put him back."

"Here, Trace," Cary says. "I'll prove I'm not infected. Give me your arm."

"Real clever. I want you to stay at least ten feet away from me at all times—"

"I can stand wherever the fuck I want to stand."

Cary gets as close to Trace as he can before Trace reaches out and shoves Cary. Cary rebounds quickly, shoving Trace back. In no time, Grace is between them, looking tired. When she says, "Trace, stop," an uncomfortable silence fills the room. Cary backs off, his cheeks pink. Trace pulls a disgusted look at the back of Grace's head.

"Would you stop acting like you want to fuck the guy?"

Grace's face turns white. She whirls around and Trace steps back, knowing at once he's crossed the line but not knowing at all how on the mark he is.

"Grace, I'm—look, Grace, I'm sorry. I know you wouldn't—"

"You should be," she says before he can finish, and there's something beyond hurt in her expression. She shares everything with him but she can't share this.

"The radio," Rhys says. "If you're finished."

Trace walks over to the radio and turns it on. The soft drone of Tina T's voice comes through the static, familiar at first and then—different.

"Emergency shelters have been established in the following locations . . ."

My fingers tingle at the list of locations. My ears perk up at the name of only one: Rayford.

"All survivors are to proceed to the shelter nearest to them for medical processing. Shelters are equipped with food, water, military protection, and first aid. Exercise extreme caution while traveling and avoid heavily populated areas. If you encounter anyone you suspect to be infected, do not attempt to assist them . . ."

"See that, Chen? We shouldn't have attempted to assist you." Trace turns the radio off. "Help isn't coming for us. We have to go to it."

"Rayford," I say.

"Yep," Trace says.

"That's almost a hundred miles."

"Yeah."

Everyone is still. No one looks like this is good news.

"Sounds like a death sentence to me," Cary says.

"Find a car," Grace says. "Drive it out of here."

"First we have to prepare, then we have to find a car, then we have to assume that car can get us there, then we have to assume absolutely nothing will go wrong from here to there."

"Your point?" Trace asks. "You're not saying anything we don't already know. We were talking about this before you got into the fucking room."

Cary keeps going, undeterred. "We don't know how congested the highway is going to be. We don't know how bad the infection has spread. How many are out there . . ."

"We could take back roads."

"Which adds more time to the trip. There's not going to be any supplies on back roads," Cary continues. "So what happens when we run out of gas? We just die on some country road or camp out in the woods? Start a colony?"

Trace throws his hands up. "Well, what the fuck else are we supposed to do? We have to go there if we want help. That's what they said. They are not coming for us—"

"I *know* that," Cary says. "I think we should go, I just want to make sure we've thought of everything—"

"What is—" Rhys interrupts. "What is 'medical processing'?"

"It's probably some kind of procedure to make sure we're not infected, duh," Trace answers. "Are you infected? No. There, processed. Welcome to safe haven."

Rhys doesn't respond. He turns the radio on and we listen to it again. And then again. Each time we hear it, what little hope it gave us diminishes until Rhys finally turns the radio off for good.

"It feels impossible," Cary says. "Rayford."

"It is," Harrison says. I thought out of all of us, he would be the most excited, the most insistent that we leave, but he's not. "I think we should stay here."

"We can't stay here forever," Cary says. "We have to leave."

"But does it have to be today?" Harrison asks. "Tomorrow? This week? What if they've reclaimed this town by the time we get there and we never had to take that risk—"

"But it's not safe here," I say. "We still haven't found Baxter's way in."

"It's saf*er*," Harrison says. "Baxter said we should hold on to this as long as possible. We have food, we have shelter, we have water, we have some first aid, and no one here is infected."

"That water's not going to last," Cary says. "It's going to run out eventually."

"Yeah, but we don't know *when*—"

"Which could be all the more reason to go—"

"Baxter said they waited now. I don't want to go out there again. They're out there and they're waiting for us—"

"Harrison, we have to do things we don't want to—"

"You'd like that, wouldn't you?" Harrison explodes and it is so beyond anything we expect from him, we're stunned into silence. "You'd make us all go out there just so you can throw us under the bus like you did with the Caspers!"

Cary's jaw drops. His eyes dart from Harrison to Trace and I watch that realization hit him hard, that Harrison is no longer "his" if Harrison ever was.

"Where's the gun?" Cary asks. He turns to Rhys. "You have it, right?"

"No." Trace doesn't even try to keep the glee out of his voice. "He doesn't."

"How could you give *him* the gun?" Cary asks us.

"I didn't *give* him the gun," Rhys says. "He took it—"

"Great, one of these nights, I'll wake up with a fucking gun against my head—"

"Now that's a good idea," Trace comments at the same time Grace says, "He would *never!* Trace would never." She turns to him. "You would never do that, Trace. Tell him."

But Trace waits an agonizing minute before saying, "Not unless I had to."

"What the fuck is that supposed to mean?" Cary asks.

"Well, maybe you'll still turn. Maybe you're just a late bloomer."

"I don't think it works like that," Rhys says.

Trace shrugs. "A guy can hope, can't he?"

The Rayford discussion just dies. Everyone is on edge after that except for Trace. He finds it endlessly amusing to incorporate words like *bang, shoot, click,* and *trigger* in every sentence that comes out of his mouth until Cary can't take it anymore and leaves the room.

Grace sits in a corner alone, wringing her hands. All of this drama. All these little dramas. It's exhausting. She looks exhausted. I go to her and sit beside her. She glances at me and glances away and I feel bad for how I laid into her yesterday. I shouldn't have.

"I'm sorry," I tell her. "I would never say anything to Trace."

"I know but Cary might," she says. "If Trace keeps pushing it." She forces a weak smile at me but her eyes are full of worry. "And then Cary probably *would* wake up with the gun against his head. It would kill Trace if he found out."

"Cary won't tell," I say.

I don't know if that's true but she relaxes a little, lets herself believe it.

"It's not going to happen again with him," she says. "It

was spur of the moment. I just—wanted to touch someone, you know? Be close to someone. He was there. Do you get that?" I do but I don't say so. "Look at Trace and Harrison." She nods at them. They're on the couches. Trace is leaned back, his hand resting between his legs. Harrison mirrors his pose. In some extremely fucked-up way, they look like they belong. "Guess what Trace said to me."

"What?"

"He said all Harrison needs is a little *guidance.*" She sighs. "I guess that's how pathetic we both are now."

"It's not pathetic." I swallow. "When everything happened . . . like the day it happened, I was thinking about you. I thought about you a lot after Lily left."

"Nothing bad, I hope."

"Never," I say. "I was thinking about that sleepover because I really liked your family. You guys were the perfect family to me."

She laughs. "We were far from perfect. Trust me."

"I needed to believe you were," I say. "It was a good memory. I needed it after Lily left." And then, something else she needs to know: "I'm not strong, Grace."

She stares at me for a long moment and then puts her arms around me.

The thing no one tells you about surviving, about the mere act of holding out, is how many hours are nothing because nothing happens. They also don't tell you about how you can share your deepest secrets with someone, kiss them, and the next hour it's like there's nothing between you because not everything can mean something all the time or you'd be crushed under the weight of it. They don't tell you how you will float through days. You autopilot, here but not really here, sleepwalking, and then every so often you are awake.

The next moment that matters turns out to be this one:

"Do you need anything?"

I'm sitting on the cot in the nurse's room. Rhys stands in the doorway. I don't understand what he's asking until I realize I'm surrounded by first aid. Peroxide, salve, and fresh bandages to tend to my forehead with. I bring my hand to it. It's crusting over.

"I want to leave it like this," I say.

"That's not going to help it heal."

I gather the supplies and go into the bathroom. I take care of the wound. When I come out, Rhys is still there. He's stepped into the room and his hand is on the back of the chair he sat in that night, waiting for me to wake up just so he could demand answers from me. He looks me up and down and I flush, remembering what I'm wearing today. A drama department dress. It's blue, straddling that strange line between casual and formal and I felt weird putting it on but earlier I decided to give my other clothes a quick wash in the showers and now they're drying out in the locker room.

"I keep thinking about what you told me," Rhys says. "About your father. I thought . . . you got away from him. You should look at it like that. Now you're free."

"It's not about him," I say.

"You're so fucking tragic, Sloane." He pauses. "I don't think I'll go to Rayford."

This surprises me. "Why?"

"I don't like the sound of it. Medical processing."

"You're not infected."

"Yeah, but we don't know how infection works. Maybe it's changing all the time."

"You know more about it than us," I say. "You knew Baxter wasn't infected. Cary. You were right about the cold." He doesn't respond. "How do you know they get cold?"

"What did your father do to you?" he asks. "You tell me about that and I'll tell you what I know about the cold. It shouldn't be hard, right? If it's not about him."

Is this what it's like to get close to other people—you do something insane together and then you have to share everything even if you don't really want to? But I weigh it. I want to know. I want to know what he knows about the cold. I want to know what it's like. I've been close to it and I don't know what it's really like.

So I count to a hundred and then I open my mouth and a history of bruises comes out.

I tell him about how my father made a room small just by being in it. How he wasn't the kind of man who hurt you and cried after, apologized after, made promises to stop that he'd never keep after. He was a machine. I tell Rhys about how my father would check us over obsessively to make sure no bruises showed, stood me and Lily beside each other in our underwear sometimes so he could take inventory of every mark. How quickly he realized hurting Lily was hurting me, how many times she stood between us . . . how the first time he got me so badly I saw stars, I had to crawl up to my room alone, the worst it had ever been and she wasn't there and then I am telling him about how she never told me she felt trapped, that I wish she'd just told me but maybe telling me wouldn't have made it better. Maybe the only way our story can end is varying degrees of sad. And that I miss her, that I need her, and this kind of missing, this kind of need, the kind of emptiness it leaves behind is worse than waking up one day and finding the whole world has collapsed in on itself, that I was over long before it was.

I tell him about how Grace and Trace kill me sometimes, for having each other, and that's what surviving is, I think. Having something. And I think of how clever Rhys is, how he asked me one thing to get me to tell him everything else. Or maybe I knew what he was doing and I wanted to say it out loud because . . .

Maybe I needed to say it out loud.

He keeps his eyes off me until I tell him, "I wouldn't have let you die out there. I know you think I would have, but I wouldn't have."

"But you went out there to die."

"I wouldn't have let *you* die. When I saw them coming for you, I ran to you, to save you," I say. "I wouldn't have left you like that. Not like she did to me." I swallow hard. "She always said I'd die without her and she left anyway."

"But you didn't die," he says.

"I did," I say. "I'm just waiting for the rest of me to catch up."

It's silent. I wait for him to take his turn, but he doesn't. He moves close to me, close enough to bring his hand to my face. He hesitates. At first, I think he'll tell me he's sorry or he understands but these are useless sentiments and he knows they'd be wasted on me. Instead, his thumb traces my mouth, lingering on my lower lip. He presses the skin of it wonderingly. His touch is so gentle that my body's first inclination is to shy from it because it doesn't understand. He leans in. We're an inch apart and his breath is on my face. My heart is beating so loud I'm afraid he can hear it but my voice is even when I ask him what he thinks he's doing. It stops him where he is and I am so aware of how much space there is in the narrow gap between our lips.

"So it's okay for you," he says.

"If you told me not to, I wouldn't have."

His eyes search mine. "So tell me not to and I won't."

I try to find the words but they're not there.

I kiss him hard instead. We're closer than I realize and he stumbles a little but he recovers and then we're all over each other, so frantic that just as I register his hands in one place—in my hair—they're somewhere else. Rhys pulls me against him and I can't breathe, I don't want to breathe. He hisses and pulls back, brings his hand to his mouth.

"You bit me," he murmurs.

"Sorry."

He presses his fingers against his lip, checking for blood. There's none.

"It's okay. Let's just go slower with this," he says.

So we do, much slower. Too slow, I think. I don't know how I'll do this. He kisses me softly, carefully, asking permission each time. He draws me out until I'm in the same nice moment with him and we move to the cot and I want to tell him I've never done this before, that he has been my first everything so far, when his hand slips between my legs and touches me in a way I have never been touched by anyone else before. My breath catches in my throat. I tense in all the wrong places, but that doesn't mean I want him to stop. I just don't know how to let this happen. He kisses my neck and I think about how we almost died out there, we almost died out there together but we didn't and now his hand is between my legs.

I watch Rhys watch me. He watches the way my body responds to him. I lean my head back and close my eyes and every thought I've had in this place dissolves until all that's left feels electric and light. His mouth finds its way back to my mouth, to my neck. I tangle my hands in his hair and he likes that. Somehow, I know he does just like I know I like how he is touching me even though it makes me nervous, even though it makes me want to turn myself inside out.

Because it's the opposite of everything. It's . . .

He presses his forehead against my shoulder. Our breathing is uneven.

"Christ—"

A voice behind us. I know it's Trace. I don't have to look to know it's Trace. Rhys doesn't let it deter him. He kisses me once more and it's tender and sweet. He moves his hand out from under my dress and its absence is immediate.

He kisses me again and then he gets off the cot but I stay still.

"Is this for real?" Trace asks.

Rhys pulls him out of the room and then I'm alone, trying to understand everything that just happened but I can't. I bring my hand to my face and my skin is hot.

Trace told everyone.

Grace keeps throwing me *talk to me* glances. I ignore them until she finally gets the hint that I don't want to talk about it. I mean, I do want to talk about it—just not with her. I want to talk about it with Lily.

I want to ask her why she got to be with other people.

I want to know why I listened to her when she told me I

had to wait for all these things until after we were out of that house, away from our father.

She must have really thought I'd mess it up, that I'd say the wrong thing to the wrong person, give everything away for a kiss and maybe I would have, if it was all going to turn out like this anyway.

I should have.

We settle in for the night. Rhys is next to me. Trace is next to me.

I wait until it seems like everyone is asleep and then I turn to Rhys. He reaches out to me. I stare at his open hand and then I touch my fingertips to his. He grabs them, holds them tightly. I close my eyes and imagine myself with him on the cot in the nurse's room until I feel the ghost of his touch all over me, until I feel like I'm ready to climb on top of him and make it happen all over again—and then take it further. When I open my eyes, his are closed. His grip on my hand has loosened. The ache for him makes me angry at her. Both feelings compete with each other, confusing me. I don't know why they have to be so close together. I *want* but I don't know what I want. All these things I could have had, I knew I could have them but I didn't know I *wanted* them. I want, I want, I want. Every part of me is reaching for something but I don't know what it is but I know it's not Rhys and it's not her.

Short breathy gasps from the mat next to mine interrupt my thoughts. I shift a little and as soon as I do, it stops. A minute passes. It starts again and then I understand.

I wish I didn't.

Trace is masturbating.

I squeeze my eyes shut and try to force sleep and then it happens and I dream of Baxter's room. I am making my way down a row of desks filled with former classmates. They look like all the blood has drained from their bodies. They stare at the chalkboard, as still and blank as statues, but I know I could wake them up if I move the wrong way and I don't want to wake them up. The closet door at the back of the room is shaking. I hurry down the aisle until I'm pressed against the door, where I found Baxter. This is where I found Baxter but Baxter is dead. We killed him. That means what's behind the door is new. I open it and then she's there, Lily is there, falling into me. I hold her until her skin melts into mine and then I'm not holding on to anything.

I wake up, fuzzy around the edges. Rhys's wrist is draped across my wrist. I raise my head. Everyone is still asleep except for Cary, who moves around the room restlessly.

He stops when he notices my eyes are open.

"What's wrong?" I ask. "Why are you up?" He shakes his head, doesn't answer. I look at him more closely. "Did you even sleep?"

"How can I sleep when the psycho's got the gun?"

"Cary—"

He holds his hand up and then heads over to the table. He pulls the chair out and drags it across the floor so it screeches loudly and jolts everyone awake.

"What's going on?" Rhys asks sleepily. "Cary, what are you doing?"

"I have something I want to talk about."

"What?"

"Rayford."

Rayford. *Rayford.* A survivor's camp, waiting. I forgot all about it and they probably haven't stopped thinking about it. I forget my brain doesn't work like theirs do. Trace shifts beside me and rubs his eyes. I think about what I heard him doing.

I wonder who he was thinking about when he did it.

"Did you hear me?" Cary asks loudly. "I said I want to talk about Rayford."

"Yeah, we *heard* you," Trace says.

It takes a while to get it together. Everyone does the bathroom thing, changes into fresh clothes. Cary's patience wanes quickly. His eyes say he wants to throttle us, but he keeps his mouth shut. When we finally gather around the table, Trace not-so-subtly claims the seat at the head of it. Cary remains standing.

"I'm trying for Rayford," he announces.

He might as well be telling us someone's died.

"You're trying for Rayford," Rhys repeats slowly.

"I want to find out what's happened to the rest of the world. I want the military protection. I want—"

"To be away from Trace," Grace finishes.

Cary turns red. "It's not about that."

"Well, the gun stays with me. You think I'll just give it to you if you convince us to go to Rayford?" Trace leans forward. "Not going to work, Chen. Nice try, though."

"It's not about that either," Cary says. "I don't give a fuck if you keep the gun and I don't give a fuck if you go, Trace. *I'm* going. If I'm the only one, so be it."

For once, Trace is speechless. He looks at Grace.

"Okay," Rhys says. "We all want to know what's going on, we all want the protection but this isn't crossing the street. You said it yourself. We don't know if we can get a car—"

"We'll find a car."

"No," Harrison says. "No—we agreed to wait here—"

"Did we?" Cary turns to him. "Why?"

"Because it's *safe*."

"So you figured out how Baxter got in," Cary says. Harrison opens his mouth and then closes it. "Yeah, that's what I thought."

"You can't blame him for not wanting to go out there," Grace says.

"I said I don't care if he goes out there. *I'm* leaving. If you want to come with me, fine. I don't give a fuck if you stay here. I'm just telling you I'm going."

"Don't be an idiot," Rhys says. "You want to get eaten alive? Sit down and—"

"I'm *not* an idiot," Cary replies. "Outside, I could get eaten alive. Inside, I could just as easily get shot in the face by a gun-happy asshole. I'm willing to take my chances."

"So it *is* about me." Trace grins broadly. "Well, you know the way out, douchebag. Far be it for me to stop you."

"This isn't a *joke*!" Cary pounds his fist on the table. "It's a way *out*. Don't you see that? I say I want to talk about Rayford—a *survivor's camp*—and you guys have to wait until you rub the fucking sleep out of your eyes to do it? Are you kidding me? We heard that message on the radio and the last thing we want to do is leave? Is that seriously how brain-dead staying here has made us? This place isn't safe. We're going to forget how to survive, so when we do have to leave, we'll die. We'll get ourselves killed."

"So dramatic," Trace says, and at first I think Trace is right, that Cary is being dramatic, but that makes me realize Cary is right. There's nothing dramatic about this.

There is a door in this school somewhere, any second the dead could come pouring in, and we move around like it's nothing. We sent Baxter out to die and Harrison, Grace, and Trace spent the next morning in the gym playing basketball. Only three of us have looked for Baxter's way in since he was sent out. I glance at Grace and wonder if she would be sharp enough to run, to make life-saving split-second decisions. We are one degree removed from our fear now.

We've gotten used to this.

I turn to Trace. "Why did you stop running?"

He shrugs. "Didn't see the—"

He closes his mouth and doesn't finish. *Point.* He didn't see the point anymore. Cary crosses his arms, bolstered.

"You're not going today, are you?" I ask him.

"No. I need a few days to plan how I want to do this. I want to make sure I'm prepared." He pauses. "They're going to come back. Sooner or later, they'll surround this place and Russo's isn't going to explode twice. If you want to go with me, fine. But just keep that in mind—you're coming with *me*. Not the other way around."

"What makes you think I'm going to follow you?" Trace asks.

"Did you not hear the part where I repeatedly said I don't care if you do or not?"

"Are you sure Rayford is closest?" Grace asks.

It's a fair enough question that Cary crosses the room and turns the radio on.

Immediate white noise. Static. No reception.

He fiddles with the dial.

"The radio's out," he says numbly.

"Are you sure it's not the battery?" Grace asks.

"It's on," he says. "It's not the battery. The radio's stopped."

We all listen hard, like maybe there's a human voice trying to find its way through all the buzzing but there's nothing.

"That's not good," Trace says.

Harrison swallows. "Does that mean the emergency shelters—"

"It doesn't mean anything except the radio is out," Cary says, but there's an edge of doubt in his voice. "Something could have happened to the tower, that's all. It doesn't mean something happened to the shelters."

But it might mean exactly that. It feels like every *next* can only be bad things. The landlines are down, cell phones are dead, the power doesn't work. The water doesn't work. We got lucky with the tank and that's going to run out and we don't know when. Emergency broadcast is officially dead. We will never rebuild. This thing will overtake us, is overtaking us. Buildings will crumble and weeds will grow through their foundations. We'll become reanimated corpses navigating a sorry imitation of our glory days and this is why I don't understand the point in going on, why it's so wrong to give up. There's nothing left.

"Turn it off," Harrison says, because he's thinking it too. Cary doesn't. He stares at the radio and he looks so hurt that he would make this bold decision to leave and it would betray him like this. The snowy rumble emitting from the speakers only seems to get louder and Harrison starts to cry. "Turn it *off*!"

Cary snaps out of it and turns it off but I feel like I need the sound because if they hear it, they'll see how stupid they're being. How dumb it is to continue. I get to my feet and go to the radio. I turn it on again and Cary doesn't stop me. I let the grainy rush of noise fill the room while Harrison whimpers and then I turn the volume all the way up—

". . . *shelters are equipped with food, water, military protection, and first aid. Please exercise extreme caution while traveling and avoid heavily populated areas. If you encounter anyone you suspect to be infected, do not attempt to assist them . . .*"

There is a collective exhalation as Tina T's voice fills the room.

I'm so disappointed.

"You've got magic hands, Sloane," Rhys says.

Trace coughs. "I'm sure you think so."

I pretend he didn't say it. I almost turn the radio off but Cary holds up his hand and then I remember why we turned it on in the first place. We listen for the locations and the closest is still Rayford.

"You've got a couple of days to think it over," Cary says. "And then I'm gone."

He leaves the room. Rhys goes after him.

Trace, Harrison, and Grace are silent.

"Megan's in Rayford," Grace says after a minute. "Maybe she made it."

"Who's Megan?" Harrison asks.

"Our cousin."

"I don't want to go with Chen and Moreno," Trace says. "Moreno will stick his neck out for Chen before he does it for us. You've seen it yourself. Those two are one and the same and I don't trust either of them."

"But it's safer as a group," Grace says. "You can't deny that. Once we get to Rayford we never have to speak to either of them again . . ."

Trace laughs and stares at the table. "That'd be nice."

"Then that's what we'll do."

That's what they'll do. I don't know what I'll do. I leave the room and no one stops me. When I reach the hall, I try to guess which direction Cary and Rhys went in and then choose the opposite.

"Sloane."

Grace. I turn.

"Are you going to leave with him?" she asks. "Cary?"

"Yes," I say. I know I have to do that much, if they're all going.

"When we get to Rayford, are you going to stay with us?"

"What?"

"Cary and Rhys will go together. I'm with Trace and Harrison will go with Trace. And you . . . is it serious with Rhys?"

This is very, very awkward.

"Grace—"

"Because if it's serious, you'd stay with him, right? That's okay, I'm just wondering."

"I don't know what I'm going to do," I say. "I don't want to think that far ahead, you know? Who knows if we'll even make it . . ."

"We'll make it," she says. "We will. And then when we get to Rayford we're going to find my cousin Megan and then we're just going to relax and . . ." She gives me a weak smile. "It'll be good. It won't be perfect but it will be good."

"I'm sure it will be," I say.

"I want to put in a bid for you."

I blink. "You want to put in a bid for me?"

"Yeah." Her eyes are so sincere. I think you have to be a good person to the core of your soul to come across so sincerely. "When we split up in Rayford, I want you to come with us."

"What about Rhys?"

She shifts. "You heard Trace . . ."

"You don't trust Rhys?"

"Trace wouldn't want him there," she says. "After everything I've done . . . I'm not going to push. Sloane, I want *you* to come with us."

"Trace wouldn't mind?"

"Not much. He'd get over it," she says. "I mean, he said it was okay . . . so what do you think?"

I think I'm going to cry.

"It means a lot to me," I say.

"Just let me know. Soon." She gives me a quick hug and then says something terrible and wonderful all at the same time. "I've always wanted a sister."

She hurries back the way she came, doesn't look over her shoulder, doesn't see me on the verge of tears. I am so much sadder about this than I should be. I stand there and try to think through her kindness enough to picture it—me going with them or not going with them—but I can't. I can't picture it either way.

Everyone is in for Rayford.

"It doesn't matter if Trace has the gun," Cary decides. He scribbles something down in an old math notebook. "It will draw unwanted attention. I think we'll be fine with baseball bats and I saw a crowbar in the custodian's room. Good, blunt objects—"

"Don't really mean anything when you're surrounded," Rhys says.

"Well, a gun won't be much help in that case either."

"Given any thought to transportation?"

"Check every car we see. If we can find temporary shelter while we look that would be awesome." Cary taps his pen on the paper. "There aren't any outside here?"

"No," I say. "The one in the parking lot has no keys and there's one across the street, but it's wrecked."

"We'll have to keep our eyes open." He frowns. "I think we can do this. I mean, we got here in one piece and the streets were overrun. It's way quieter now. If we're lucky, most of them are still at Russo's. We'll stay away from that side of town."

"Just because the streets aren't overrun—"

"Yeah, I know. They're quiet now," Cary says. "At first I thought we should leave at night so we can be hidden, but I think it would be better if we could see any infected coming for us, don't you?" He doesn't wait for a response. "Maybe we should go just before dawn, so it's dark but not for long. Oh, and everyone needs a pack full of supplies. Two packs to two people was a stupid idea. We could get separated easily. We might have to separate."

"You really want to do this as a group?" I ask.

"If you're all coming, you're all coming," he answers. "I would've done it alone if I had to but there's an obvious strength in numbers."

I think of the Caspers then, of Harrison. I know I shouldn't. I shouldn't let my mind go there but I do. If he had never been with Lily—is that the thing that saved me? That made him choose Harrison over me? Being her sister? If he had to make that call again, would he choose

Trace out of spite? Or maybe Grace. Maybe Grace would be the one. I can't stand the idea of that happening to Grace.

"Sloane, I know what you're thinking," Cary says, watching my face. "And I wouldn't do that to either of you."

But it's not either of us that I'm worried about.

"We trust you," Rhys says.

I glance across the room. Harrison is napping on the couch. I look at him and the only thing I can see is how dead he's supposed to be. I wonder what it would be like if we'd gotten here without him. Less tearful, maybe. I wonder if we'd cry for him.

"Harrison could be right," I say. "By the time the water in here runs out, the military could be reclaiming cities. Towns. It could be over by then."

"I'm not staying here with Trace longer than I have to," Cary says, keeping his voice very low. "I don't trust him and I will never trust him."

"But you'll let him leave with us," Rhys says.

"He'll have other things to worry about than me out there."

"What do you think, Sloane?" Rhys asks.

"I think we'll probably die," I say.

Cary closes his notebook. "Very uplifting."

Later, Rhys asks if he can talk to me alone.

He asks me in front of everyone, when we're at the table, eating. *Can I talk to you? Alone?* I say yes and it isn't until Trace dog-whistles when we walk out together that I think maybe Rhys doesn't actually want to talk at all and then I feel cornered by the idea of touching him and him touching me. It has to happen, doesn't it? If it's happened twice before.

We haven't even been on a date.

And then I wonder if I owe him anything after what we did, if I have to touch him first. If it's my turn to figure out how to make him feel electric. I have no idea how I'd do that.

We circle the building slowly, not talking. Every so often I catch him looking at me and there's a question in his eyes each time he does but he doesn't ask it and I can't stand it, so I ask mine first.

"Do you want . . . do you want something from me?"

"What?"

"You want . . . something. Right?"

"What? No—Jesus. I just wanted to talk." He sounds as flustered as I feel and I'm glad it's too dark in the halls for him to see my face clearly.

"What do you want to talk about?" I ask feebly.

"I just wondered if you thought . . ." He pauses. "I mean . . . do you think there's anything human left in them?"

I think of the dead girl on top of me. How empty she seemed.

"No."

"So do you think they have souls?" The way Rhys asks it is different from the way Harrison asked it, like he's not just idly wondering, but he really needs to know. "Because they die, but they come back."

"The first death. The soul must go with it. They're not people, Rhys."

"How do you know that?"

"Because I'm God."

This actually gets a laugh out of him, a small one.

"I can't stop thinking about it. They look so sad when they turn. Just in that second after. They look like they know what's about to happen but there's nothing they can do . . . and then the light goes out. But that's why I wondered—just that second . . ."

"Your parents turned," I say. "Didn't they?"

I think I've always known. I wait for him to confirm it. He feels my eyes on him and he crumbles a little. At first, I think he'll cry. He brings his hands to his eyes and stays so still and then he takes a shuddering breath out. When he lowers his hand, there are no tears.

"You were supposed to tell me how," I remind him. "How you knew . . ."

So he does.

"The night . . . before it all really went to hell, a group of dead got into our house. Like six of them. We thought it was a break-in and one bit my dad. We got upstairs and locked ourselves in my parents' bedroom and we called the police. The police came." He pauses. "They were overwhelmed and we knew something had gone wrong, but not what or how, so we just thought we'd wait it out in the room until it was safe or backup came. We barricaded the door. My dad was like—he was sick, but we thought he was just upset . . . and then he said he felt cold."

I wonder what infection feels like from the inside. If you can sense yourself becoming ice. And your emotions and memories too—they become ice, and you turn and then you're free.

The way I'm thinking about this is still all wrong and romantic . . .

"Near the end, he said he didn't want to hurt us. It's like he knew it was . . . it's like he knew it was taking him over. And then his heart stopped. And then he came back. He bit my mom and I knew what I had to do. The only thing we had in that room were his golf clubs." He takes a deep breath. "Her bite wasn't so bad. She was lucid . . . longer. I thought maybe if it was small, it wouldn't count. But in the end she got cold too."

"You killed them both."

"I didn't even wait for her to turn," he whispers.

I remember how covered in blood Rhys was. All over his shirt, his jeans, caked on his neck, his hands. I didn't even think about it then, but it must have belonged to his mother, his father. For seven days, he wore their deaths and he never said a word to any of us about it. I feel so bad for him and I don't know how to tell him, so I reach for his hand and hold it as hard as I can, crushing his fingers in mine. It's a futile attempt to redirect his pain. He lets me hurt him for a few minutes before gently pulling away.

"It was so easy," he says. "Just physically . . . doing that. When it was over, I thought . . . people . . . we aren't made of anything. That's how easy it was."

"I'm sorry, Rhys," I say.

"It's okay."

"It's not okay. It's horrible. It's—"

"No," he says. "It's fine."

"Why?" I don't understand. I want to understand. "Rhys, why—"

"Because I'm here because they're not," he says. "So I have to make it mean something." I don't say anything and he shakes a little, like he's trying to get the nightmare off him, like that's possible. "Are you coming to Rayford?"

"I don't know," I say. "Grace wants me to go with her."

"Grace *is* coming with us."

"I mean when we get to Rayford. She wants me to stay with her and Trace. After."

Rhys nods slowly. "I'm sure that invitation doesn't extend to me or Cary . . ."

"It doesn't."

"Are you going to do it? Are you going to stay with her?" he asks, and I don't answer him because I don't want to answer him. I think he's putting me between them but I'm not sure. Nothing like this has ever happened before. "What if I wanted you to stay with me and Cary." I don't say anything. "Sloane, are you going to stay at all?"

What he really means: am I going to leave. Am I going to finish the plan I came here with, the one I wrote down and carried with me, but have failed to see through again and again.

I open my mouth and then I close it as quickly.

"Tell me what happens next," he says. "Just tell me."

"I don't know."

"You won't stay for Grace and you won't stay for me," he says. "You wouldn't even stay for yourself. Just Lily, right?"

"Rhys—"

"Who left you," he says like I don't know this or that he knows it better than I do but he could never know it better than I do. I'm starting to wish I'd never come out here. And then he says, "She wasn't the one who was trapped." He lets this pronouncement hang between us like somehow it's going to give way to some sort of personal epiphany or an undoing. Like I'll become light with that knowledge, like I never knew it before. He tries again. "If you're staying, I want you to stay with me." I want so badly to ask him why, why he thinks he needs me, but he continues. "If you're not staying . . . if you're going to go through with it, wait until we're out of your way. I couldn't stand to see it."

"Okay," I say.

"I really hope I don't see it, Sloane," he says softly. "I really hope you wake up."

He hesitates and then he brings his hand to the crook of my elbow. He presses his lips against the side of my mouth and my heart recoils because for all its gentleness, it hurts.

He goes back to the auditorium alone.

So we prepare.

We go through lockers and find book bags for everyone. There are certain requirements: utilitarian is best. They can't be too big or bulky or easy to grab. We overstuff them with water bottles and food and find them too heavy and then we start making hard decisions like less water or less food? Medical supplies. We need those too, in case someone gets hurt. It quickly becomes obvious we'll need far more than we'll ever be able to carry.

In the end, the book bags become a depressing sight lined up in the library.

"We should go with the clothes on our backs," Grace says. I don't think she's talking about the latest ensemble she's wearing. Another fifties-style dress. "Layer."

"Good idea," Trace says. "It's not exactly warm out."

"Hey," Cary says. "We made it seven days out there before—"

"You mean most of us made it seven days out there before."

"Okay, *most* of us made it seven days out there before." He gives Trace a bitter look. "We should probably establish some ground rules for that gun."

"Sure." Trace nods. "Rule number one: you don't get to tell me how I can use the gun. Great. I'm glad we had this talk."

"Trace," Grace says. She turns to Cary. "What were you thinking?"

"Gunfire will draw them out. Any loud noises will. Don't use it unless you absolutely have to. That's all I was going to say."

Grace turns back to Trace. "Use discretion. Sounds reasonable."

Trace gives a grudging shrug. I look around the library. Walls, ceiling, doors that are locked and barricaded. Soon we'll be trading them for the ugly outdoors. I can't help but feel a certain nervousness about what's coming the day after tomorrow.

On the way out of the library, Grace asks me if I've thought about what I'm going to do when we get to Rayford. I tell her I haven't and she looks disappointed. I know it's awful and ungrateful to leave her hanging after she can say something as extraordinarily generous as *I've always wanted a sister* to me but I am afraid to tell her yes. I can't promise to stay with her when I don't know if I will. I couldn't do that. I'm not like Lily.

Still, the guilt I feel about it is like a thousand needles all over my skin and it doesn't go away. It lasts through dinner, after dinner, after the sun sets. I take a shower in the dark to get it off me. The cold water hurts, but it's a better hurt.

Soon there will be no more showers, none. Nothing.

I sit on the bench in the dark, naked. I run my hands over my body, feeling out my bruises without being able to see them, and I think about what Rhys said, how we're not made of anything. I wonder if my father felt the same way about me, Lily. Maybe once he realized it the first time, he wanted to realize it over and over because it made him feel like he was made of something. I get dressed slowly and make my way back.

The halls are pitch dark. I let the flashlight guide me but I go the long way around, taking corners, pausing at exits, studying the barricades we put up.

I keep walking, letting the light trail over the floor.

My heart stops.

I jerk my hand up, washing the ceiling with light. I think I must have been imagining what I just saw, like I've imagined my father's cologne and I have imagined his voice. I did not just see—what I thought I saw. I squeeze my eyes shut and count back from ten, until I've calmed down and then I direct the ray of light from the ceiling, over the wall. It spills into the open basement door.

The open basement door.

My hand shakes. If I don't move, if I don't move the light, if I keep the light off it, it will go away. I open my mouth to shout for help but if I shout for help, I might wake it.

The body on the floor.

I aim the light back on it and in the time it took me to do it, he is up, on his knees, his palms pressed against the floor.

He stares at me. The expression on his face is odd. The fresh clothes I last saw him in are tattered. He is filthy. He left here clean and came back filthy. Came back *alive*.

"Mr. Baxter," I whisper. "Mr. Baxter, what are you—"

"I told you I wasn't infected," he says. "I told you."

He reaches for me.

I run.

I know it's stupid dangerous to turn my back on him, that I shouldn't leave him in the hall but I have no other choice. I burst into the auditorium and I'm shouting, *Baxter's here—he's here*! And no one asks me if I'm imagining it this time. Trace gets the gun from wherever he's been hiding it and there are more flashlights, spastic beams of light dancing all over the room. I tell them what Baxter said to me before I fled. *I told you I wasn't infected. I told you.*

We storm down the hall, around the corner to the place

where I found him, and I expect him to be gone but he's still there—like I first saw him.

Flat on his back. Crumpled.

We stop.

"Mr. Baxter?" Cary calls.

We wait for him to move, respond. He doesn't.

Cary steps forward but Trace cuts in front of him, the gun out. He holds it over Baxter's prone, still form. Cary goes to the basement door and peers inside.

"Why did he come back?" Harrison asks. "Why?"

"He's not infected," I say. "He can prove it. He wants shelter."

Grace kneels beside him. Baxter's eyes are half-open, glazed. He blinks and moves his lips but no words come out. She leans forward.

"Mr. Baxter? Can you hear me?"

"We can leave him here." Trace lowers the gun. I step in front of him and crouch behind Grace. Trace circles Baxter until he's behind us both. "We're going. He can have the school."

"Holy shit," Cary says softly. "Did you see this?"

He runs his flashlight over the floor, revealing the dirty gray tile. It's streaked with blood. He follows the trail all the way back to Baxter and I can't figure out what part of him it's coming from, what part of him is open. Baxter closes his eyes.

He stops breathing.

"Oh, God," Grace whispers. She brings her fingers to Baxter's neck to feel for his pulse. She looks up at us. "He's cold."

"Grace," Rhys says. "Get away from him—get away from him now—"

I pictured this differently in my head. Pictured the turning slow. Baxter starts breathing again. Relief flashes across Grace's face until she notices the difference. The terrible familiarity of the sound creeps up on her. The mechanical breaths of the dead.

Baxter's body jerks once.

He opens his eyes.

His irises are white.

"Grace, *get back!*"

Baxter grabs Grace and in one swift motion, their positions are reversed. She's on the floor, on her back, and he's on top of her and someone is screaming, everyone is screaming—

"Get him off her—get him off her *now!*"

Grace pushes at his shoulders, tries as hard as she can to get Baxter's mouth away from every part of her flesh and then Harrison shouts, "Trace, *the gun!*"

But I don't think there's time, there is no time. Baxter grabs her wrist and pulls it to his lips and I do the only thing I can think of to do—I grab Baxter and I pull him off her and then there's a shot, this incredible *bang* and it's so in my ears I feel it in my teeth. Baxter rolls sideways and I go with him, but he is not dead. It wasn't a good enough shot. Baxter starts to twitch my way and I'm frozen but if this is it, it's okay because I saved Grace. I saved her.

"Sloane, *move!*" I don't know who shouts it. Cary, Rhys, Trace. There's another shot, another shock, and then,

Baxter is motionless on the ground. Trace's aim was true this time.

Blood pools onto the floor from Baxter's head.

"*Shit!*" Trace is shaking. "You said he said he wasn't—you said he wasn't infected!" He says this to me like this is my fault. Like I brought Baxter back into this school. He stares at the gun for a minute. "I killed him," he says stupidly. He laughs. "Holy shit, I killed—I—*fuck*! That was close—Grace—" He turns to her. "Grace?"

We all turn to her.

She's still on the floor, dazed.

Trace hurries to her. "You didn't get bitten, did you? Did you—"

"No . . ." She tries to get to her feet but it's like invisible hands keep her pinned to the ground. Her eyes widen in faint surprise. "Oh . . ."

Trace sets the gun down and a dull whine fills my head, my heart breaks in half. His hands hover over her like he's afraid to touch her and Cary shines the light on her slowly and I see red, her stomach is red.

"Oh Grace," I say. "Grace—"

"I'm okay," she assures us, and she tries to get up again but she can't and her eyes settle into a kind of understanding that makes me want to run so far away.

"No," Trace says. "I didn't—I didn't—" He pulls her upright into his arms and she cries out and he moans like her pain is his. She buries her face in his chest. "Talk to me." He shakes her a little. "Grace, talk to me. Please."

This didn't happen. This is not happening.

"I don't want to die," she says.

I step back. Rhys wraps his fingers around mine, stopping me.

I can't feel it.

"Okay, don't talk if you're going to say things like that." Trace squeezes his eyes shut. "I'm sorry—I am so, so sorry, Grace—"

"Don't be mad," she whispers. "Please don't be mad at me."

"I could never be mad at you," he says, and she starts to cry because it's all she can do, the last thing she'll ever do. "Grace, come on."

"Please don't be mad." Her voice is getting smaller and smaller. "I don't want to do this to you . . ."

"Then don't—come on, don't do this to me—you don't have to do this to me . . ."

But she does. Grace dies in the hall, in her brother's arms, in our school in this stupid, unforgiving world where there are no phones or ambulances or hospitals or doctors. She closes her eyes and she tries so hard to stay, but in the end she lets us go.

Trace asks to be left alone with her body.

We wait for him in the auditorium. No one speaks. We try, but our voices sound funny when we do, our words awkward and stiff as they fall from our tongues, like we are just learning to talk. It is hard to hear anything over the ringing in my ears, the beating of my heart, the air entering and leaving my own lungs.

Harrison is curled up on his mat, crying.

I want to hurt him until he stops.

Seconds pass, minutes pass, hours pass. The sun rises. When Trace finally comes in, we are all so much older. His eyes are red and swollen and his face is drained of color. There is blood on him—Grace's blood stains his shirt, his pants.

Even knowing this, I look for her. I look past him for her. She's not there. Half of me understands this but half of me refuses to believe it and that half of me is waiting for her so we can talk about this. We can't talk about her being dead without her being here.

Trace looks at us and no one says anything.

There is nothing any of us can say.

Seeing him makes Harrison cry harder. He covers his mouth and sobs. Grace kissed that mouth when she was alive. Cary's mouth. It hits me again: Grace is dead. Just like that, there is no Grace. We live in a world without Grace.

"Where is she?" Rhys finally asks.

"I took her to Ms. Yee's room," he says. "She's there."

My eyes drift to Grace's mat. Where she should be. Some of her things are still scattered around. The clothes she wore yesterday. Rhys asks if we can see her and Trace tells us no. He crosses the room to Grace's mat. He picks up her sweater and buries his face in it. He starts to cry and the material can't muffle the sound. We sit there and watch him uselessly until he raises his head.

"This is real, isn't it? That happened." And then he calls her name. "Grace? I—"

There is no answer.

He stares blankly at nothing and then he grabs her blanket, her pillow, and walks out of the auditorium. The air is too heavy to breathe. I can't breathe. I get to my feet and I leave and I walk down the hall, my hand against the wall to steady myself because the world is moving, it's moving under my feet until I finally have to stop and just sit on the floor. I don't know how long I'm there before Rhys is beside me, helping me stand.

We walk back to the auditorium together.

There is a window in the basement we never barricaded.

This window is at the back of the school, facing the athletic field. It's close to the ground and semi-concealed by boxwood. That's how Baxter got in. It would be a forgivable oversight except as soon as Cary tells us about it, we all see it in our heads and it is the most painful kind of realization. The next stupid thing: shelves were placed in front of that window, a barricade. Baxter put them there the first time and then fought them down the second but don't worry, Cary tells us, nothing else found its way in after Baxter came, after Grace died.

We checked that basement and we looked at those shelves.

"It wasn't obvious," Rhys says, like that should make it okay that we looked at those shelves and never considered the possibility of a window behind them. It actually makes it worse. We all knew Baxter was lying about forgetting, he wanted to use it as leverage so why wouldn't he hide it from us? Why wouldn't we look for something hidden?

"Where is he?" Rhys asks. "Where did you put his body?"

"He's in the basement." Cary stares at his hands and then he shakes his head. "I can't believe he came back just to do that."

"We sent him outside to die," Rhys says. "Why can't you?"

"Someone should check on him," Harrison says. "Trace, I mean."

"You do it," Cary tells him. "You're closer to him than we are."

Harrison's eyes widen. "I don't want to—I don't want to see her—"

"You wouldn't."

"That's not fair."

"Yeah, well, he can't stay in that room forever. We have to go to Rayford."

"Jesus," Rhys says. "He just lost his sister, Cary. Give him a couple of days."

"You think he'll still go with us?" I ask.

Cary shrugs.

"I'll check on him," I say.

I leave the room without looking back. Each step forward is a slow and hateful thing. I am going upstairs to see Trace, who is sitting with Grace's body. I bite my lip and tears come. I think the worst part is knowing it hasn't really sunk in yet. This is just the surface of it, like when Lily left. First there was the shock, this total implosion, and then numbness and every so often it would hit me in waves, just to remind me it was still there. Each wave was worse than the last. A full-body ache, this heaviness, seeing the world in gray.

I'm standing outside of Yee's classroom when I hear Grace's voice.

She's talking to Trace.

Relief surges through my veins, makes me weak. I *knew* it was a mistake, some unreality. I knew she was alive. I *knew* it. I push the door open and it slams into the wall. Trace sits on Yee's desk and my eyes pass over him in search of Grace but they don't see her how they expect to see her. They come to rest in the middle of the room, where all the desks are pushed together to display—her. She's covered with a sheet, but her voice—

I still hear her.

I turn to Trace. He's holding the camcorder.

My heart crashes.

"We made a video," he tells me because he doesn't know I know. "In case . . ." He pushes a button and Grace's voice stops and the room gets colder as soon as it does.

"The battery will run out soon and then I'll never hear her again."

The air tastes funny. Strange. Everything is different now. The school is so alien. You'd think this place only ever belonged to us, that it was always ours and it is something so much less with one less of us in it.

"Can I see her?"

"You don't want to see her." He holds up the camcorder. "You can see her here. Alive."

I walk over to him, never unaware of the other presence in the room. I don't know how he stands it. I sit next to him, lean in close, and stare at the tiny LCD screen. It's paused on the two of them.

The quality isn't that great. It's fuzzy. Trace didn't adjust the settings for recording at night and the only thing illuminating them is the flashlight and it makes Grace look unreal on top of unreal. I have this urge to find my way into the video, to tell her what's coming. *Grace, did you ever imagine that you'd die.* He turns it off and looks at me. His eyes are empty.

"Do you need anything?" I ask. "I can get you . . . anything."

"No," he says. "You can't."

It gets quiet again. And then—

"Do you think if we brought one of those things in . . . if we brought one of those things in and they bit her . . . she'd . . ." His voice cracks. "Do you think she'd come back?"

"No," I say, my stomach turning. "No. She wouldn't. It's too late . . ."

"Were you going to stay with us?" he asks. "She told me she asked you. Were you going to?" My mouth goes dry. "Don't lie to me. Just tell me if you were."

"I wasn't sure."

"She really wanted you to come. I wasn't so sure but she liked you."

"I know."

"She said you didn't know if you'd go because of Rhys."

"It wasn't because of Rhys."

"But she really liked you." It's almost an accusation. I don't say anything. He rubs his eyes. "If I step out for a second—will you stay with her? I hate when she's alone . . ."

I nod. Even so, it takes him a long time to leave. His entire being resists it. I can see the fight happening in him. He finally steps out. Leaves me alone with her. I know he'll be quick so I know I have to be too, which means there is no time to prepare. I hurry to the center of the room, the desks, her body.

I grip the edge of the sheet and pull it back.

This is what true death looks like. She's not infected, so she will not turn. She's so gone from us no bite will bring her back. I bring my hand close to her face, but I can't bring myself to touch her. Everyone says death looks like sleeping, that it looks like that kind of peaceful, but this is nothing like that. The stillness. Her lips, her mouth, her hair. Everything is wrong. I can't accept that she's here in this room, in front of me, but she's not here. She's here but she's not. I think of the dead outside, bodies. Bodies— but not *people*.

But they were people.

I cover her face. When Trace comes back, he finds me next to her and I just want to say something that will make him feel better, less alone. Remind him he still has family.

"Go to Rayford. Find your cousin."

He looks at me. "Leave Grace, you mean."

"I didn't mean it like that—"

"How else could you have meant it?"

"Trace—"

"Get out. I want to be alone."

"I'm sorry—"

"Get the fuck out, Sloane! Who told you I wanted you here in the first place?" He gets so close and for one second, I think he'll hit me. I see my father. I will see my father in every anger. *Get out.*

I brush past him and as soon as I'm out of that room, I can breathe in a way I couldn't before. My legs are shaky. Weak. When I go back to the auditorium, Cary and Rhys are waiting for me.

"How is he?" Rhys asks.

"Bad," I say. "Where's Harrison?"

They don't answer.

"What?"

"Tell her, Cary," Rhys says. He doesn't sound happy.

Cary flushes and clears his throat. "He wouldn't stop fucking crying and I kind of lost my temper. He's wandering around. Did you mention leaving to Trace?"

Rhys looks at me. "Tell me you didn't. It's way too soon to throw that at him." My face gives it away. He closes his eyes. "Shit, Sloane."

"That's Trace's problem," Cary says. "Not ours."

Rhys gets up abruptly, throws Cary a disgusted look.

"I'm going to find Harrison."

When Rhys is gone, I just stand there, staring at Cary.

"Grace is dead," I tell him.

"I can't bring her back."

"She was ours and she's dead."

He stares at the table.

"She wasn't mine."

"But you were with her."

"Sloane." He looks at me and the bags under his eyes are pulling his face down. In the right light, I'd swear he was infected. He exhales slowly through his teeth. "Don't."

Thoughts of Grace prevent me from sleep.

I doze, thinking of her body in Yee's room, decomposing. We probably can't move it from there without something happening, her skin shifting. I don't know where we'd move it. I just think we need to do something with her.

It doesn't seem right that there can't be a burial.

I think about how no one has said anything about her.

We haven't talked about how she was good, that she was nice, that she loved Trace more than anything in the world. These things still matter. She was a good person. She wanted me to stay with her when we got to Rayford. The memory of that fragile possibility of her and me, me being part of the kind of family I always wanted to be part of—I feel the weight of it like it's still there, even though it's gone.

I wasted it.

The room gets light. The sound of quick, heavy foot-steps nearing wake me completely. I open my eyes and see Trace striding across the room. Nothing about him being away from Grace makes sense to me and I have that dumb thought again—*she's alive*. It's the only way he'd leave her.

"Trace—"

And then he kicks me. In the side. My head spins, my bones scream. I wrap my arms around myself at the exact same moment he aims for my abdomen. His foot connects with my arm instead. I groan. I can't breathe. He brings his foot back and kicks me in the legs. I roll away from him. He kicks me again and I split in half.

"Trace—Trace—*Trace!*"

Rhys and Cary are awake. They pull him away and Trace starts screaming.

"I had the shot—I had the fucking shot and *you ruined it!*"

I force myself to my feet and stagger across the room. I lean against the stage and try to get my bearings. He had the shot. I ruined it. I frantically sort through images in my head, trying to remember. It's not true. I pulled Baxter off

Grace, I pulled him off of her, there was no time—the shot, there was the shot, but I saved her I—*I jump between them. I grab Baxter and pull him off her and then there's a shot, this incredible bang and it's so in my ears that I feel it in my teeth.*

I sit down on the floor.

He had the shot and I ruined it.

Trace stops, just lets himself go right there. Cary and Rhys struggle to hold him up but his weight is too much for them. They ease him onto the ground and he starts to sob. Rhys hurries over to me, reminds me of the pain I'm in but it's not anything. It's not real.

Trace's pain is real.

"Help him." I want to scream it though; *help him.* Help Trace, help Trace. Please. Harrison and Cary stare at him uselessly. "You should help him—"

"I can't," Rhys says, but I think he must be wrong. There must be some way to help Trace. We just haven't thought of it yet. "Are you okay? Did he break anything—"

I stare at Trace and it already feels like a lifetime ago that he hit me, made me see stars, my head against a coffee table, blood in my hair—no, wait. That wasn't Trace.

"Sloane," Rhys says. I shake my head slowly. He takes my arm. I try to pull away again. "Let me see how bad it is."

I hear Lily's voice in my head. After, she'd always tell me to *just calm down. Let me see how bad it is.* Did he break anything. No. Does anything feel broken. Yes. But not bones. I would know something like that, right, Lily? I'd know it. He'd never break anything, he'd never do a thing that would force us to the hospital because no one could know. No one can know what he does to us. Wait. That's not Trace. Trace. I ruined his shot.

"He's right," I whisper, and Rhys stops looking me over. He sits down and rubs his eyes. Cary pulls Trace to his feet and says something about taking him to the nurse's office.

Just calm down, let me see how bad it is.

They don't just put Trace in the nurse's office. They lock him in it.

I take a shower. At home, the showers after would be so hot, they'd turn my body to mush and I'd wrap myself up in my oversized terrycloth robe and lay on my bed and sometimes Lily would sit on the edge of it and I'd go so quiet, it scared her. She'd stay there, whisper about all the things we'd do when we finally got out, just her and me.

I change back into my clothes. Zip up my jeans. I slip out of the locker rooms and make my way to the nurse's office. I peer through the window. Trace is on the cot, on his back, staring at the ceiling. I can't tell if he's awake or not. I rap my knuckles against the window. He doesn't move. I think of Grace, laid out on the desks, the exact same position as him and she's not moving, not seeing, not breathing. Time has stopped for them both. I press my hand to the glass and will his head to turn, for him to sit up, say something.

He stays perfectly still.

I go back to the auditorium and I'm alone for a moment.

And then footsteps. Rhys, Cary, Harrison. I don't want to see them right now. It's why I took the shower. I couldn't stand the way they looked at me, like I was this pathetic weak thing. There's no time to leave the room, so I climb onstage and slip behind the curtain.

"She wasn't in the locker rooms—"

Their voices get closer to the stage so I back farther into it, wedging myself between the old out-of-tune piano that's there and the wall. My hands brush something plastic. I look down.

My phone.

I stare at it for a long time, trying to remember how it got here, trying to remember the last time I was behind here with my phone.

Rhys running his hands all over my back, telling me I'm fine . . .

"There aren't many places she can be."

"We couldn't even find the fucking way Baxter got in."

"Let's just keep looking. Harrison, check the back of the school."

They leave the room again but I stay where I am. I turn my phone on. It turns on. The last phone in here that works and it's useless. There's no signal.

But I have a text message.

I have a text message.

It's the end of the world and I have a text message.

We've been in the school a little over a month but the message is dated three days after the morning it all started. I don't know what I was doing then. Where exactly we were. We were a group. The Caspers were alive. Grace was alive. Text messages were still going out.

It's from my father.

I tremble so badly the phone shakes in my hands. Beads of sweat blossom on my forehead and the back of my neck. I can't get air into my lungs. I lean forward, hyperventilating, praying somehow to regain myself. *It's old. It's old. It's an old message. It's old, it's old, it's old* . . . and then I laugh stupidly, dizzily, because his timing is so—it's so good. It is so good. *It's old,* I think firmly, but another thought is louder and it makes me want to break myself, it makes me want to end it all here, now: *he's alive.*

I open the message.

Lily's here. It's safe. Come home.

PART FOUR

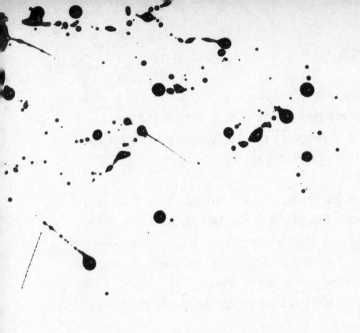

I need to go.

I get to my feet and jump down from the stage. I need to go to her. I need to get home *now*. No—I need to make sure I'm seeing this. I walk out of the auditorium, trying to figure out which way Cary and Rhys went. My hands are numb, still shaking so badly that I drop my phone. It clatters to the ground. I crouch down and pick it up, make sure it's okay.

The message is still there.

And then my legs decide to stop supporting me. I sink to the floor and press my hand against my forehead and I start to laugh and then I start to cry.

"Sloane?"

I lower my hand and look up. Rhys and Cary are at the end of the hall. They rush to me, asking questions, *what is it, what happened, what's wrong.* They try to guess. *Are you hurt? Is it the barricades?* They'll never guess. I wipe my eyes and hold my phone out to them.

"Do you see it?" I can barely get the words out. "Do you see the message—"

Rhys takes the phone from me. Stares at it. He hands it to Cary wordlessly. Doesn't he see it? I can't tell if he sees it. Cary frowns and then his mouth hangs open in disbelief. I think he should be as ecstatic as I am in this moment—the girl he loved is alive and doesn't he want to see her of course he'd want to see her—but instead he says, "This is old, Sloane."

"It's not that old," I say. "We have to stop there before we go to Rayford. We can get her and then we can all go to Rayford—"

"You don't even know if they're alive—"

I rip the phone out of Cary's hand. "It says it's *safe.* It's safe. We can stop there and we can get her and we can go to Rayford. My dad—he has a car—"

"They could be gone if they've heard the radio—"

"*No.* They're still there—she wouldn't leave if she came back." She went out of her way to leave me. If she came back, she means it. She means it this time for good. She has to. "She wouldn't leave if she came back this time. She wouldn't do that to me—" They exchange a glance and I want to grab them both and shake them, something. "It doesn't matter! We're going to Rayford anyway—we can stop there. Why can't we stop there?"

"No one said we couldn't stop there—"

"Why am I asking you permission?" It hits me so hard. We don't have to do everything as a group. "I don't have to ask you if I can go to my *home*. I'll just go there myself—"

All I wanted to know was if they saw it, if the message was real. It is and I'm packed. I can leave. Cary grabs my arm and it's the wrong arm, the one Trace kicked and something about that brings me to my senses, turns me back into the Sloane I was and have always been, except I don't want to be her because she fills my head with this thought immediately: even if we find each other again—

"Calm down," Cary tells me. "We can go, Sloane. Of course we can check it out."

She still left me.

I push the thought out of my head.

Bury it.

We decide to leave in the morning. There's no point in waiting anymore.

Cary asks me if I want Trace to come with us, like it should be up to me, like I would even think of leaving him behind when he's Grace's brother and they'd already decided to go to Rayford, where their family might be. He has to come.

"If she'd said no, were you just going to leave him in the nurse's office?" Harrison asks.

"He's coming," I say. "Stop."

"Someone has to tell him what's going on," Cary says. "Harrison, that's you."

"What? Why me? I don't want—"

"*Christ.*" Cary buries his face in his hands for a long moment and when he finally raises his head, he looks ready to kill Harrison. "If I'm dragging your sorry ass through Cortege, you can just do what I fucking tell you. You know why you've never done anything that matters? Because you never *do* anything. Tell Trace. *Now.*"

Harrison leaves the room with tears trailing down his cheeks and I understand why he's afraid to see Trace. Trace's grief and anger mark him now. But Harrison made his choice.

"I'm going to divide Grace's—" Cary takes a breath, trying to collect himself. "Her book bag. I'm going to divide everything inside it between us."

"Okay."

He goes to the library and thinking of him opening up her bag, everything she was going to take with her, makes me so sad and I try to think of Lily instead, seeing Lily, but it doesn't help. Rhys watches me from his side of the table. There's nothing in his eyes. His mouth is pinched.

"What?" I ask.

"I'm happy for you," he says.

"Thank you."

"I hope she's there."

"She will be."

He nods but he doesn't say anything and I know he doesn't believe me, but I don't care because I know it's true. Lily will be there.

"When we went outside," he says, "if it had worked out the way you wanted it to . . . you would have never seen the message. Or her. So I guess it's good it didn't work out." I look away. "And your father's there. You'll see him."

"He's dead," I say.

"How can you know that?"

"He's dead to me. If he's alive, we're not taking him with us."

"It's his car, isn't it?"

"I don't care."

"I'm happy for you," he says again.

But I think he means it less and less each time he says it.

Cary comes back and then Harrison comes back and tells us Trace has agreed to go but he wants us to pay our respects to Grace before we do and then I realize every time I envision us leaving through the library, she's there. She's with us, she's alive. I erase her from the mental image but that feels so wrong so I let her stay, but I try to make her look like a ghost instead.

Which is worse.

I spend the evening on my mat staring at the skylights, watching it get darker and darker. I'm starting to feel everything Trace did to me and I'm afraid it will slow us down but I think if you want something bad enough it can be greater than pain, it can push you past it.

I hope.

"Sloane."

Rhys whispers my name. At first, I'm not sure I'll answer him, even though I'm awake but then I think what if he dies? I'm trying not to consider all the things that could go wrong, but what if he dies and this will be the last moment I share with him. I owe him more. I roll onto my side to face him. He's staring at me. I wonder how long he's been staring at me.

"We should be asleep," I say.

"Are you scared?"

I shake my head. It's a lie and it isn't. I'm not scared right now. I'm not scared in the way that he must be. He looks so vulnerable when I say no, so upset, like he's the last scared person in the world and he doesn't want to be alone with that.

"I'm jealous of you," he whispers. "It kills me to look at you."

"Come here," I tell him. But there's not enough room on my mat for him to just be close to me. He moves his next to mine and then we're lying together. I bring my hand to his hair, which is soft. He smells like smoke. He curls into me, puts his arms around me. It makes me wince. He loosens his grip immediately.

"I'm sorry."

"It's okay."

I take his arm and I put it around me again. He closes his eyes. I let my fingers trace the outline of his face and his lips. His breathing is ragged, broken.

"Sloane," he says.

"What?"

"When we get to Rayford can I stay with you and her?"

"Of course," I whisper. "Of course you can."

He starts to cry. I pull him closer to me. He presses his face against my collarbone.

We fall asleep like that.

Trace stares at us through the window.

His eyes are hollow and his jaw is set. Cary unlocks the door to the nurse's room and pulls it open. I stay behind Rhys and Harrison. If I'm afraid of anything right now, it's Trace. I don't want him to lose it on me again. When I woke up this morning, everything hurt a little more and I *have* to be able to run. He makes no move toward me. There's no anger on his face but that doesn't mean it's not there.

He steps past us and then he stops and I know we're meant to follow. We make an unconscious line behind him, a funeral procession. The only thing missing is the coffin but I feel the weight of it. Her body inside. We shuffle up the stairs, our footsteps in eerie unison. We reach the second floor. He hovers on the landing. We hover with him.

The hall is dark.

He takes a deep breath and moves forward.

We are ten feet from Yee's room when he stops again.

We wait.

Nothing happens.

"If I go in that room," Trace says, "I won't come out again."

Even though he hurt me, even though he thinks I killed her, I don't want him to go in there because from here, I see her in him. I never saw it when she was alive but now I do. The shape of his face. His eyes. The way he moves. It's not as delicate, but it's her.

It makes me feel like she's not dead.

He brings his hand to his mouth, considers it. I know he could easily stay here forever with her. He turns to us. His eyes fall on me and I shrink away.

"Lucky," he says. It's all he says.

We follow him back downstairs, to the library.

The barricade is down. It's raining again. Cary says that's a good thing. It will be an uncomfortable thing, but maybe the rain will mask our scent, keep us invisible when we need to be invisible. He hands out our weapons. Rhys and Cary and Harrison take the baseball bats but Trace refuses one. He lifts his shirt, revealing the gun, and then raises his chin, daring us to say something but we don't. I take the crowbar. I need the weight. I lace my arms through the straps of my book bag. The other thing I'm taking—my note to Lily. I want it with me even though I don't plan to die before I see her again. Not now.

"We're going to jump the fence," Cary says. "We'll go through the trees until we're directly across from the alley—" The alley. Where Mr. and Mrs. Casper died. "And we'll just keep cutting across street after street, every goddamn shortcut until we hit Sloane's house."

"What if we need to stop?" Harrison asks.

"Hopefully we'll have somewhere to do it," Cary says. He turns to Trace. "Don't fire the gun unless you have to. From here on out, no talking. No shouting. No panicking."

All of these things sound sensible.

If we do these things, everything will be okay.

But that's not how it really works.

He doesn't ask us if we're ready. There is no real ready for this. He just looks at each of us and when he isn't met with resistance, opens the door. My heart seizes. It's still too early, too dark. Dark enough not to see our own deaths coming and I haven't once imagined a death that was out of my control since this started. I tighten my grip on the crowbar.

The rain falls. Heavy drops hit the building, the path. The trees beyond the path. Those trees are bare. They'll offer little to no cover but it's better than nothing.

I turn back to the school.

Running water. The walls, the ceiling. The barricades. Our fortress.

I turn back to the open door.

My sister.

I'm the first to step through and it feels like I'm step-ping into a dream. The path is clear and the trees ahead are clear and Cortege is quiet, quiet enough for me to question whether it ever happened. The boys follow me. I bring my hands to the fence and remember the sound it makes when you go over. I slide my crowbar between the chain link.

We line up against the fence. I squint. There's nothing in the distance. I think of Baxter. *They wait.* They wait, but they can't be invisible. I climb the fence. The metal is slick and cold and the book bag feels awkward against my back, but I'm first to reach the other side. I take their base-ball bats and set them quietly on the ground, one by one, and then we make our way through the small thicket of trees, our footsteps crunching against dead leaves from last fall. Still, there is nothing. No sign of them. I look at Cary, Harrison, Rhys, and Trace. They're uneasy, heads swivel-ing in all directions, like the silence is noise. I hear them breathing.

I look back at the school again.

Good-bye, Grace.

We reach the middle of the brush. Cary holds out his bat and points to the street, urging us forward. The alley. My hair is wet, my clothes are wet. My palms are sweaty. The Caspers. The poor Caspers, dead. We trudge into the street.

The open, empty street. The sky is lightening.

"Maybe they moved on," Harrison whispers.

Cary throws him an angry look for speaking.

I point.

The alley is empty but it's not empty. There are bodies. I see at least three of them spread out along that narrow concrete path. The ones who turned and were put down. Rotting on the pavement. I search the road and my vision opens up to other shapes.

At first glance, they look like lumpy debris, but they're bodies.

The real dead.

Rhys taps the ground with his bat. We look at him.

"Run for it," he says.

Run. It would be stupid to go out there slowly hoping not to disturb anything. Rhys holds up three fingers and lowers one at a time as he counts down.

Three . . . two . . . one.

I push forward, out of the trees, my book bag scraping against outstretched branches, escaping their feeble attempts to grab at me. My feet hit a puddle off the curb of the road and the splash is deafening. The water soaks my ankles, my jeans. We're a stampede of the living. The alleyway is so close I can taste it. We hit the middle of the street and—

The bodies seem to get up at the same time.

I stop. Stop. Stop.

"Stop!"

I don't know who yells it, if it's me, if it's one of them. We stand in the middle of the street, backs to each other. My head spins at the sight of all the bodies rising stiffly to their feet. Rotting faces, the dead who have been out here, waiting. Skin slipping off, entire layers of it gone or melting into nothing. Organs on the outside, crusted and dried to clothes, remoistened by the rain. New dead, ones who have been freshly opened and are oozing everywhere. Women and men, girls and boys. People I might've known but can't recognize anymore. There is every shade of blood— black, brown, red, pink. All eyes looking at us through that same milky film that sees us for what we are and what they are not anymore.

Trace raises the gun.

"*No,*" Cary says. "We need to run—"

"Where the fuck are we going to run?" Rhys asks.

Our voices incense the infected. They charge at us and Cary goes left, forgetting the alley, the shortcut. We follow after him. My side aches at the effort but I can't quit before I've started. I can't. The dead are fast behind us and I can hear them screaming but it's not like we scream—it's a strange, high-pitched, thin screech, like a noise trying to make its way through crushed vocal cords. I want to stop and curl up in the middle of the road and let whatever happens next happen, that's how scared it makes me.

"The park," Cary shouts to us. "The park—"

But I see something better.

"Cary, that car—"

It's across from the park. I veer away from them, run to it. It looks in good shape, a small yellow four-door. A gift from God. Rhys and Cary scream my name. The boys straddle the middle of the road but they never stop moving. I pull on the door handle and the shrill whooping of the alarm explodes into the street, louder than anything.

"Shit—"

I stagger back, rejoin them. We run into the park. I pretend I don't see the overturned truck in the sandbox, the bright pink coat of a dead little girl under a swing set. Garbage cans on their sides, garbage everywhere. Cary points to the public bathrooms and we run to them. He pulls the door open and we step inside. It swings shut.

"No lock!" He pants, feeling for it. "There's no fucking lock!"

The stench hits us then. A sour, biting scent invades my nostrils and makes me gag. Rhys coughs. We turn. Two closed stalls face us.

I push open the one on the right and then I recoil. What was a man is sitting on the toilet slumped over. There is a hole in his head and his body has been ravaged, bite marks, missing chunks of flesh everywhere, revealing muscle and bone. Dried blood cakes the floor.

Harrison starts to heave.

"Harrison," Cary says. "Harrison don't you dare—"

He doesn't. No lock. There's a small window at the back of the room intact. We could climb out of it. I turn back to the door we pushed through, waiting for an onslaught of dead to filter through, to trap us in this box, but it doesn't happen.

"What are they doing?" I ask. "Why haven't they come in yet?"

Cary hands me his baseball bat. He creeps over to the door and opens it up the tiniest bit, enough to see through. I bring my shirt collar over my mouth. The combined smells of the bathroom and the rotting corpse makes my eyes water, makes me want to spend the next thousand years vomiting up my own guts. Cary closes the door and turns back to us.

"They're at the car. The alarm. More are coming. We have to get out of here before that alarm stops—" He searches the room and sees the same window I did. He climbs onto the sink and peers out. "This side is clear, I think. We go out this window." He pushes at the frame and nothing happens. "We're going to have to break it."

"Then what are we going to do?" Harrison asks.

"Find a place."

This side of the park slopes down, a hill stopped by a tall wooden fence that separates it from Hutt Street. Hutt Street is the closest thing we have to suburbia. It used to be a field and now it's being developed into a bunch of houses that look the same. A few are for sale, some are sold, and some are under construction. One of them has to offer temporary shelter.

"Sloane, break the window," Cary says.

It takes two tries to break the window with the crowbar. The first time it recoils and only cracks the glass. Second time's the charm. It shatters. I try to clear away as much of the broken pane as I can but Cary tells me to *stop, stop it we have to go*. Except the window is too small to fit through with our book bags on. We toss them out ahead of us and then we squeeze through slowly. I go first, after the last book bag. The glass cuts into my arms and I think of that woman twisting her way through our picture window. The picture window. How can it be safe at home if the picture window is broken?

Rain spatters against my face. I land on the ground. There are no dead here, but I don't know what's beyond that fence. Harrison is next out the window and then Cary. As soon as he's clear, an ominous rumble sounds overhead. The sky opens up and drenches us.

We have to crawl down the hill so we won't be seen. We drag ourselves across muddy, dead-spring grass. It's a full-on storm and the only thing I'm grateful for is the smell of earth this close to my face. I dig my hands into the grit. I like how it feels.

Even amid all this, I like the way it feels.

I don't know how long it's been since we left the school. It's light out now. It can't be that long but maybe it has been. Time has a way of shifting funnily in situations like these. There is not enough of it or there is too much of it and it's always one when you need the other.

We finally get to the edge of the fence and press our backs against it. We can't stay here long. Sooner or later, the dead will drift from the car—the alarm has stopped—and stumble their way down here. And the fence—it's not the kind you can jump.

I press my face against it, like I could hear through the wood, through the rain. I can't hear anything. I don't know what's on the other side. I hate to gamble like this.

We crawl along. Trace is in the back. Cary is in the front. I'm behind Cary, Rhys is behind me, Harrison is behind Rhys. Lily will freak when she sees me like this, covered in mud, alive. I wonder if she'll cry, if she'll believe I'm there, if she'll press her hands against my face to prove it. I bet even then she still won't believe it.

Cary stops and I'm so caught up in thoughts of my sister, I run into him. We've reached the end of the fence. He holds his hand up. *Wait.* And then he crawls forward, forward, peers around cautiously. After a minute, he moves even farther around for a better look and then he jerks back, pressing himself against the fence.

"There's a group coming up the other side," he says. "They're going to make their way around in a minute. We have to move or they'll see us. We'll get to one of those houses and lay low until the rain lets up. Ready?"

We get to our feet and curve around the fence. The sight at the opposite end of it is sickening. A group of infected converging, turning their heads searchingly. The ones who reach the fence first paw against the wood. They seem to know we're around but not where. Cary gestures us forward and we are quiet but we are not invisible and I wish we were invisible. The houses across the street are invitations. Their doors are open, open mouths.

We need to run.

We just need to run for it.

We don't. We tiptoe across that road, the rain silencing our footsteps. We go to the first house we see and hurry up the steps.

The door is locked.

Cary looks around and then jumps over the side of the porch and we follow him between two houses. I know what he's thinking. *Maybe there's a back door, maybe there's a back door. Maybe it's open.* Harrison sticks close to Cary. I'm next to Rhys. Trace hangs back.

We've almost cleared the house when the rain turns into glass. I feel it in my hair and against my face. Broken window. An infected has jumped from a window of the house beside us. It lands neatly between us and a scream rises in my throat but dies on my lips. Rhys pulls me back and we stumble into Trace. It's a man. A dead man. Not long dead, I don't think. His skin is gray, tinged purple, and his eyes see everything and nothing. There are gashes on his hand. His neck is wide open. He rasps air at us, momentarily confused to be surrounded by so many living. He turns slowly, his steps stilted.

He faces Cary.

Chooses Cary.

Cary charges into the dead man and they both go flying

into the ground. I raise my crowbar over my head to bring it down on the man before the first bite can happen when I realize it's not Cary. It's Harrison.

Harrison jumped in front of Cary.

I slam the crowbar into the man's shoulder. It doesn't stop him. The man grips Harrison's shoulders, pulls him down, and bites into the first piece of flesh his mouth can find—Harrison's cheek. I could fool myself into thinking it's a kiss, but then the skin separates from Harrison's face and it's just red, a river of red dragging down his face, hanging flesh, and the dead man pulls at it with his teeth, annoyed it's still attached to the person it belongs to.

Harrison screams and I'm terrible because the first thing I think is he's going to draw attention, not that he's doomed, that he's going to die one way or the other. Rhys raises his bat. Blood spatters, brains everywhere. Like that, it's over. I look behind us. Nothing else has come.

Yet.

Rhys kicks the dead man off Harrison and Harrison lays on the ground making fish-out-of-water noises, twitching, shocked. We surround him. His mouth moves, open, closed, open, aggravating his wound, making the bleeding worse. He's trying to say something but nothing is coming out. Cary bows his head as close as he can get it to Harrison's mouth. Harrison's eyes go wild and then he finally finds his voice.

"There," he says.

Cary looks up at us. His face is wet. I don't know if it's just the rain.

"Get in the house," he tells us.

"But—"

"Get in the house!"

We crawl in through the broken window, leaving Harrison and Cary outside. I fall onto a cold kitchen floor and crawl across it, past an island, before getting to my feet. The house has an open layout, a kitchen that bleeds into a living room that opens down a hall. Stairs. I don't see any dead but I see bloodstains everywhere. The TV screen-down on the floor. An overturned table with missing legs. Ripped couch.

I clutch the crowbar and step forward cautiously as Rhys and Trace fall in behind me. Rhys runs to the front door to make sure it's locked. Trace makes his way up-stairs. I make my way to the other side of the house, into what looks like an office. Empty. The windows are all shuttered. I meet Rhys in the hall. Trace pads halfway down the stairs.

"Is it clear?" Rhys asks him.

Trace nods and goes back upstairs and I realize he hasn't said a word since we left. I move to follow him—I don't know why—but Rhys grabs my arm and holds me back.

A clattering noise sounds from the kitchen. We go to it and find Cary on the floor, on his hands and knees. The baseball bat rolls in front of him. He has two book bags.

No Harrison.

"Don't say anything," he says.

He stays like that for a long moment, trying to gather the will to get to his feet. It isn't until Rhys makes his way to the window that Cary manages to stand.

"Don't look out there," Cary says. "I'll cover it."

My stomach turns. I watch Cary struggle to move the fridge in front of the window. Rhys and I offer to help but Cary refuses to let us. I wonder what he's thinking, if he's thinking of how it was supposed to be Harrison when we were first outside. How Harrison was so worried about doing nothing with his life but in the end, he gave it to Cary. Harrison, dead. I'm filled with pity for him but I can't say I'm entirely sad. I move to the wrecked couch and shrug off my book bag. I sit down. I'm immediately aware of how cold and wet I am, how sore. I close my eyes and listen to the rain.

Harrison and Grace are dead.

The couch depresses. Someone sitting beside me. I can't bring myself to open my eyes again. I keep them closed. The body in the bathroom. Mr. Baxter. Lily.

When I open my eyes, I feel time has passed. Rhys is on the opposite end of the couch, his face pressed into one of its pillows. I dig into my book bag and pull out one of the water bottles. I polish off half of it before I even think about conserving. I shove it back into my bag and look around. Cary is at the kitchen table. The baseball bat rests in front of him. He rolls it back and forth slowly. I make my way over.

"What's it like outside?" I keep my voice low.

He shrugs. "They know we're around. They're on both sides of the street now. I can't get to any of the cars. We'll have to leave."

"Do you have a plan?"

"Run. Hope for the best. I should tell Rhys to get it together." He pauses. "And Trace. He's upstairs. He won't come down."

"I'll get him," I say.

"Be careful."

I linger there for a minute and instead of going straight for Trace, I sit down beside Cary and he moves away from me. I reach for his arm and he pulls it back. He doesn't want anything I'm offering.

I leave the table and walk down the hall, climb the stairs. I search the halls for Trace. I find him in a bedroom. Someone's bedroom. A dress hangs over a desk chair. A slew of family photos are pasted onto the wall and all seem to center around one young, blond girl. This must be her room.

Trace sits on the edge of her bed, looking out the window. The gun is in his hand. He runs his thumb along it. He turns to me and fear squeezes my heart until his expression softens, becomes something very sad, and then I'm not afraid anymore. It would kill her to see him like this. If she can see him like this now, it's killing her.

"I'm sorry," he tells me.

I sit down on the bed. He returns to the view of the street below. I follow his gaze and I see the infected walking slowly back and forth.

"It's okay," I say.

"Okay," he says. He nods. "Good."

He puts the gun under his chin and pulls the trigger.

Blood is in the air. It's in my mouth.

I stumble away from Trace and then Rhys and Cary are at the door asking me what's going on and then they see it and understand it immediately. Trace is dead. We've lost Grace, Harrison, and Trace. There are only three of us now. Only three.

Rhys grabs my arm and tries to haul me to my feet. "We have to go—" He pulls me away from Trace's body but I dig my heels in because Grace wouldn't want me to leave him like this. "Sloane, we have to leave—"

"But—Trace—"

"No, we have to go *now!*"

I glimpse the view out the window. The infected are scrambling, trying to source the sound of the shot. I can hear a familiar thudding echoing through the house. Splintering wood. We rush downstairs and I am trying to explain how Trace died, he killed himself, even though they know. I run into the living room, grab my crowbar. I try to get my book bag, fumble to put it on but Rhys and Cary are screaming that there's *no time, no time*. The fridge teeters forward and back, the dead trying to push it out of the way. They know we're in here.

"We're close," Cary says as we follow him down the hall, "so just *run!*"

He pushes the door open. I know this, we've done this before, those first few days. The streets bustling with hungry dead, us against them, no time to think up a better plan than *just run* and hope and pray. I take the lead and I make them sprint for a house across the road—it's Mrs. Crispell's house. The backyard is fenced.

"We have to get past the fence—"

I'm hyperaware of the uneven footfalls behind us, the animal growls. We've lost the numbers game. We are going to die. Still, we press on, we reach the fence. The boys fight their way over it. I'm last to go, half over the side when one of the dead grabs my sneakers. It bites into the sole of my shoe. I scream and kick at it blindly until I connect with something soft and mushy and it finally lets go.

I hit the ground, land on my side, the wind is knocked out of me. For a second the world wavers and I think I'll black out. If I do that, I'll die. Rhys and Cary are way ahead, they're running ahead. They won't stop for me, won't help me up. They can't. I have to do this on my own. Lily . . .

I force myself to my feet, staggering dizzily for a second before my head clears. The fence rattles behind me. I look back. A group of infected shake at it, try hard to push it down. They are so hungry, so desperate for us that they can't make their bodies understand they need to climb.

I run. This street, Gunter Street, is less crowded. I see cars but there's no time to stop. I pass by a house, searching for Rhys and Cary when I spot them crawling under the back deck of Mrs. Schmidt's house. I crawl in after them. We get lucky. We're not seen. We keep pressed to the ground and stare at the street ahead, the last street before mine.

There are dead everywhere, milling around.

We'll never make it.

"Maybe they'll clear," Rhys says weakly. "If we wait."

So we wait.

We are under that deck for hours, none of us talking. I have all these things I want to say about Trace bubbling up my throat but I know it's not the time.

It's just that he's gone.

He was here and then he was gone.

Like that.

More time slips away as we wait for the dead to find something better to do. They don't. They're waiting for us and they could wait forever. They have forever.

We don't have forever. I'm numb and my body aches. I feel like my mind is dying. We're going to die out here in the dirt, waiting. Rhys moves close to me. Somehow, he's not cold. I huddle next to him. We can't stay here all night. If we stay here all night, we'll stay here the next night and the night after that.

"That's the Seals' yard." I point to the house across from us. "All we have to do is go through that house and then mine is right there, across the street."

"Easier said than done," Cary says.

"We have to do something," Rhys says.

Cary thinks about it and then he says, "We split up. I'll go right, you and Rhys go straight through. If we all head in the same direction, they'll close in and it's game over."

"We meet at Sloane's house," Rhys says.

"Right." Cary pauses and then stares at me. "So look after yourselves."

I know then. I am more sure of it than I am of Lily being at home, waiting for me. I know he is going to go right and if he makes it, he'll keep going. I want to change this, but all I do is reach over and squeeze his hand.

He squeezes back.

He elbows his way out from under the deck and then he starts *shouting,* telling them to come get him. The dead pursue him immediately, don't see Rhys and me wriggling out from under the deck. We don't actually see if Cary makes it—but he made it, he had to make it, I know he did.

And that's how we say good-bye.

Rhys and I stumble through the Seals' backyard. We

catch the notice of four infected as we clamber up the steps to the back door. It's open and we throw ourselves through it. I slam it shut and lock it. The dead throw the full weight of themselves against it. It's not going to hold.

Rhys leans against the wall, catching his breath. I don't want him to catch his breath, there's no time. I am so close to her, I can feel it. I grab his hand. It sounds so ridiculous, so delusional, but I know we're safe in here. I know the path is clear for us from here on out. I know I will get where I need to go and I'll see her. I drag him to the front door, stare out the window.

My house. The yard is clear. And the picture window—

"The windows are boarded," I whisper excitedly. "The windows are boarded—" Another thought crosses my mind. "But the doors probably are too—"

The back door starts to give. They're going to get past it. I fling the front door open and grab Rhys's hand again, forcing him forward. We trip down the steps and race to my yard. I push on the front door but it won't open. I step back and notice the second floor windows are clear. I bet she left them clear for me. Rhys follows me around the side of the house. The maple tree outside my window. My grip tightens on the crowbar.

"We have to climb it."

Our desperate scramble up is nothing like in the movies. The bark is gritty and painful against our hands and the rain has made it slick. There's no learning curve. Lily is the one who climbed trees, not me, and I think that's the only reason I make it. Because I know she did it.

Somehow, we get to the weak branch that leads directly

to my window. By that time, the infected are below us. The branch strains under our weight and starts to give as I break the glass with the crowbar. I launch myself through the window. Rhys falls in after me. I crawl across the floor and use my bed to get myself to my feet—*my bed*—and I'm dizzy with how untouched my room is. The end of the world didn't happen here.

Or maybe it did. Maybe I'm dead. I turn to Rhys.

"We made it, right? We're here—Rhys, are we here? Rhys—" I crouch next to him and put my hands against his face while he gasps for breath. "We're here, aren't we?"

"We're still here," he manages.

Home.

I stand in the middle of the room wondering why she hasn't come to meet me. The house is boarded and safe but I broke glass. I broke glass and I hit the floor hard, but no one has come up here to investigate. The door to my room stays closed.

Maybe they're in the rec room and they can't hear me.

Maybe they heard me and think I'm death and they're hiding from it.

"How is Cary going to know to climb the tree?" Rhys's voice is raspy. He looks at me. "He won't know."

My throat gets tight. I don't say it, but he sees it in my eyes.

Cary is not coming back.

Rhys buries his face in his hands.

I can't ignore the feeling building inside me that something is wrong.

"I'm going to check the house," I say.

Maybe my father lied. Maybe Lily was never here and this was just his way to get me back home. I tighten my grip on the crowbar, which makes my other hand feel too empty, so I search for something I can put in it. I pick up a piece of my window. Glass. It's jagged, but feels right with my fingers curled around it.

Rhys gets to his feet but I say, "I want you to stay here."

"Sloane—"

"Just stay here."

He won't win this and he knows it. He sits on the edge of my bed—*my bed*—and tells me to shout if something happens. I nod. I move across the carpet, leaving muddy footprints in my wake. I open my bedroom door quietly and close it just as quietly behind me.

The hall is empty. Movement catches the corner of my eye. I whirl around and confront—my reflection. The mirror at the top of the stairs. I drop the glass and touch my face. I am caked in mud and my hair is straggly and knotted from the rain. My lips are bruised. There are cuts and scratches on me that I must have gotten since leaving the school but I don't remember how. She won't recognize me when she sees me. I look like someone who has survived.

I bypass the stairs, my heart thudding in my chest, and go straight to her room. I'll know what I'm dealing with if I do that, if he was lying to me. I close my eyes before I open the door. I pray. I wasn't raised to believe in God, but I am not above begging favors. I open my eyes.

The sight brings tears. They streak through the dirt on my face.

She's been here.

I know she has. Her bed is rumpled, it's been slept in. I almost cross the threshold but I remember how dirty I am. I don't want to get mud on her floor, her things. I run downstairs and nearly fall down the last three steps.

"Lily? Lily—"

I pass the living room. The picture window is covered, boarded. The glass cleared away. The front door has been nailed shut. Our street must have cleared out quickly for him to find the time to do this. I stop when I reach the kitchen. The breakfast table. *You better eat that.* The room is empty. The house feels like a ghost.

What if they went to Rayford.

I hurry across the room and push the door to the garage open.

The car is there.

I close the door and step back into the kitchen. Keys on the hook beside the fridge.

They're not in Rayford.

"Lily?" I call, softer this time.

I walk back down the hall with the memory of my father's arms on me, pulling me to the rec room. I let them take me there again and press my hand against the closed door. I know she's inside. I open the door and peer into the dark. A weak yellow glow radiates from the edge of the room. A flashlight, I think. I walk down the stairs, stand still at the bottom of them.

My eyes travel over the mess. The overturned chair. The desk at the back of the room. My father's desk. The TV in the corner—the screen cracked. Something happened here but it doesn't matter because in the middle of it all, in the heart of this room, is a blond girl with her back to me. She stiffens.

"Lily," I say.

She turns.

Gray skin. Angry veins. A dead girl's face. The side of it is peeled away and rotting. The corners of her mouth are red, her lips black and crusty, her eyes sunken and white. She opens her mouth and runs at me, her arms out, she pushes me, throws herself at me and I use the crowbar to keep her back. She digs her nails into my shoulders, while I keep the metal pressed against her throat.

She doesn't feel it, doesn't choke against it.

She's cold.

I force her off me. She gropes to her feet and lunges at me again and I meet her this time, this time I'm on top of her, using the crowbar to keep her pinned against the floor by the neck. I hear something inside of her crunch against the pressure.

"Lily," I say. "*Lily*—it's me. Lily—"

She thrashes under me and then suddenly she stills, seems to focus. She sees me. Her eyes get wide and there's something in them—I think there's something in them but I don't know what and I try so hard to understand it; *I'm sorry, I can't do this anymore.* Tears spill over my cheek and drip onto hers. The look in her eyes fades. She digs her hands into the sleeves of my shirt and grinds her teeth together. Her gaze flickers around the room as she tries to figure out a way she can be free from me, always. Even though she knows I'll die without her.

But maybe that's how it's supposed to be.

I drive the crowbar into her face.

I disappear into a dark, empty place.

There is nothing to see, nothing to feel. It's a relief to be in something so endless and undemanding because everything has been too much and I've been so tired. I hear my heartbeat in this place, steady at first, but eventually it slows and then it stops.

I wait.

Sloane.

I open my eyes. My arms are wrapped around my dead sister's body and my head is resting against her chest and the voice that has pulled me from the darkness, without my permission, belongs to Rhys. He's above me and she is beneath me and she's not moving anymore. I uncurl my fingers from her and he helps me to my feet and I stare down at my sister's dead body and its stillness wraps itself around my heart and it fills my lungs until I want to bury myself inside her. I want to bury myself inside her.

"Sloane, we should—"

The gritty sound of air cutting through dead lungs sounds from the other side of the room and pulls my gaze from Lily. My chest tightens. More dead. Close.

I don't know how there could be more.

I point to her and then I hold my hand out. Rhys takes the crowbar out of her face, a sick, awful sound that becomes a part of me as soon as I hear it. We cross the room slowly and a familiar scent floods my head with images, puts a bitter taste in my mouth, makes me want to tear my skin off . . .

I find my father on the floor, wedged between his desk and the wall. His eyes are cloudy, his skin is gray, his veins vivid, so visible. He's on his back and his abdomen is wide open, but it's been so feasted on, it's hardly there anymore. What's left of his insides are dried out, have cemented him to the carpet. He flails his arms uselessly but he can't get up.

Lily did this.

I raise the crowbar over my head. I'll finish this. Everything. But his teeth—they catch my eye. They're perfectly white, clean. They've never sunk themselves into anything. He's weak and his expression is sick with want. He moans at us. I lower the crowbar.

"Just leave him," I whisper.

We go back upstairs. Rhys packs clothes and searches the house for supplies. I take the car keys and shove them in my pocket and my fingers brush over a crinkled piece of paper. I take it out and unfold it. My note to Lily. I stare at it. It's been through as much as I have and the letters have smeared together, have mixed with dirt and blood.

Only a few words are readable now.

Rhys steps into the room. "Are you ready?" I stare at the letter. Can't stop staring at the letter. He moves in front of me and brings his hand to my face. "Sloane, are you ready?"

I open my mouth but nothing comes out. He tells me he should drive. I give him the keys. The car starts on the first try and the gas tank is half full. He lets the car idle while I open the garage door and then I run back, jump into the passenger's side. He eases out of the driveway and then we're moving and we go by empty, broken houses, abandoned cars, and then eventually, the YOU ARE NOW LEAVING CORTEGE sign. We pass more dead along the way and they reach for us before they know we're gone.

"Tell me what happens next," Rhys says after miles of silence because he knows. He knows the brief moment where everything was certain—her, me, him—is over now and I don't know what's left anymore. I turn my gaze away from him, back to the window. I catch sight of something.

I tell him to stop and he stops.

A young dead girl limps across an otherwise empty road. She's so little. She can't be more than seven. Her ankle is badly broken but she drags her foot along determinedly until she finds herself at my window. She puts her hand to the glass and I do the same. Her palm is so much smaller than mine. She's too young, too frail to break through what separates us but she stares at me with pure longing. Her eyes are so desperate.

I see them in her.

Lily. Grace. Every death I've ever known is in her eyes and they are looking out at me, all of them, reaching for me with more than just this animal need to consume. It's more than that. I don't know what it is, though. But I need to know.

"Sloane," Rhys says.

"Wait," I whisper.

I move closer to the glass, as close as I can get to it, begging her, begging Lily, begging Grace, begging all of them to tell me what's left, to just *tell me*, while the girl pushes against the window, turns her tiny hands into tiny fists, begging me for a taste of—*life*.

My life.

Lily disappears. Grace. They all leave, they're gone, they will never be here again. But the weight of what they've shown me is settling into my bones. I don't know if I will keep it, but just in this moment, however brief, I feel closer to it than I ever have before . . .

The dead girl presses her face against the glass. She waits for me to tell her what's next.

ACKNOWLEDGMENTS

For their love and faith in me: Susan and David Summers, Megan and Jarrad Gunter, Marion and Ken LaVallee, Lucy and Bob Summers, and Damon Ford.

For working hard to bring this book together, inside and out: Amy Tipton, Sara Goodman, Lisa Pompilio, Anna Gorovoy, and all at St. Martin's Press.

For their kindness, keen-eyed critiques, and inspiration: Emily Hainsworth and Tiffany Schmidt.

ACKNOWLEDGMENTS

For their listening and encouragement: CK Kelly Martin, Nova Ren Suma, and Daisy Whitney.

For the very first push in this direction: Mur Lafferty.

For the helpful e-mail about the phones: Brian Stoffer.

For their support and zombie-related enthusiasm: Kelly Jensen, Robert Kent, Will and Annika Klein, Amy Spalding, Brian Williams, TS, and every single one of my friends and readers.

For their lovely hearts and minds and for sharing them with me: Whitney Crispell, Kim Hutt, Baz Ramos, and Samantha Seals.

For more than I could ever say in this small space: Lori Thibert, TF. NRSM4L. (Shake it out!)

Thank you all. Without you, this book would not have been written.